Someday,
Somewhere

Someday, Somewhere

Lindsay Champion

KCP Loft is an imprint of Kids Can Press

Kids Can Press gratefully acknowledges the financial support of the Government
of Ontario, through the Ontario Media Development Corporation.

Published in Canada and the U.S. by Kids Can Press Ltd.
25 Dockside Drive, Toronto, ON M5A 0B5

Kids Can Press is a Corus Entertainment Inc. company

www.kidscanpress.com
www.kcploft.com

The text is set in Minion Pro and Didot.

Edited by Kate Egan
Designed by Emma Dolan

Printed and bound in Altona, Manitoba, Canada in 1/2018 by Friesens Corp.

CM 18 0 9 8 7 6 5 4 3 2 1
CM PA 18 0 9 8 7 6 5 4 3 2 1

Library and Archives Canada Cataloguing in Publication

Champion, Lindsay, author
Someday, somewhere / written by Lindsay Champion.

ISBN 978-1-77138-931-0 (hardcover)
ISBN 978-1-5253-0042-4 (softcover)

I. Title.

PZ7.1.C43Som 2018   813'.6   C2017-903831-1

For Mom, my favorite writer

First Movement
Adagio sostenuto ~ Presto

{ I }

Dominique

"Get it, Dom! That one. Go, go, go!"

I hurl my backpack onto a seat in the third row, and behind me, Cass cheers. There are slashes in the brown pleather and white stuffing is puffing out, but mission accomplished: we're sitting right near the door, I won't get sick from the back-of-the-bus exhaust smell and we're nowhere near Anton and his asshole friends. Triple jackpot, three cherries.

"Damn," Cass says. "You should be in the Olympics for bag throwing. Cyd Charisse."

"What?"

"You said James Cagney at the end of lunch. Cyd Charisse."

Everyone's still pushing down the aisle, so I look around to make sure no one else is listening. Cass and I are always in the middle of an epic round of this game — I don't even remember where we learned it. Basically, one person picks a celebrity, and the next person takes the first initial of the celebrity's last name (so, C for Cagney) and says a new celebrity, whose first name starts with that letter. We play it with old Hollywood stars, and it's the only thing that keeps us from losing our freaking minds at school.

"Cary Grant," I say.

"Gene Kelly."

"Katharine Hepburn."

Pause.

"Damn it."

Longer pause.

"Do you want a clue?" I ask.

"No."

"You sure?"

"Yes." Pause. "No." Cass punches the seat in front of us. "Fine, give me a hint."

"*Once Upon a Time in the West.*"

"Oh! Henry Fonda."

"Yep."

"Okay, your turn."

Easy. Frank Sinatra, star of *Guys and Dolls*, my third-favorite movie musical of all time. But I always beat Cass at this game and I don't want him to feel bad, so I take a few minutes to pretend I'm thinking.

I turn to face the window, letting my eyes blur as boarded-up row houses zoom by. In an hour we'll be in our favorite place in the world. New York City. It's the first thing Cass and I ever bonded over, in fourth grade. Our teacher, Miss Calcott, asked everyone in class to go around and say what we wanted to be when we grew up. Most people said a vet or a basketball player or whatever, but I said I wanted to be a modern dancer with the Alvin Ailey American Dance Theater in New York. My mom and I watched them on TV once and it was the most magical thing I'd ever seen in my whole life. There was this one dancer with long, curly hair who kept twirling in the air, and I knew instantly that she was exactly who I wanted to be. Cass told the class he wanted to be a firefighter. Then at recess he took me behind the basketball court and confessed that he wanted to move to New York, too, and be an actor. But he begged me never to tell anyone, because the other guys all wanted to be firefighters and he thought they might not want to be friends with him anymore if they knew.

After that we started going to my apartment almost every weekend to watch old movies together. I'd play him all the ones with great dance scenes, like *Seven Brides for Seven Brothers* and *West Side Story* and *Singin' in the Rain*. His favorite of all time is *Casablanca*, so that's why I call him "Cass" — well, not when anyone else is around. His real name is Chris, but that just doesn't fit him. The *real* him.

There was one year in middle school when we spent every weekend searching thrift stores for a long trench coat just like Humphrey Bogart's in the movie. He'd try a coat on and pop up the collar and make his eyes all squinty, and that's how we'd know if it was *the* coat or not. But when we finally bought one at the Salvation Army, he never even wore it. He just kept it hanging there in his room, next to the blue bathrobe his grandma gave him for his birthday. Which is funny, because he's one of the bravest guys I've ever met. You wouldn't think a six-foot dude in a big black sweatshirt with a diamond stud in his ear would care what other people think of him. But deep down, he does. More than anything.

And me. Everything about me is a happy medium — well, medium. Happy is debatable. I'm just a medium-sized, moderately attractive person (I *guess*, even though I'd never actually admit to anyone I think that) with a middle-of-the-road personality, and look where it's gotten me.

The middle of a school bus.

Anton lets out a gross, rumbling burp that makes my stomach feel full of curdled milk. I whip my head around to the back of the bus to face him. He wiggles an eyebrow, the one with the three notches shaved into it, and smiles. I look down, skin burning, eyes stinging, mortified I even let him catch me glancing in his direction. I don't care what he does and I don't want to give him the satisfaction of thinking I do.

Then there's an old, familiar smell — a sweet-sour chemical smell that burns the inside of my nostrils. I instantly know what he's doing. He's melting the back of the seat with his lighter. I've seen him do it a million times when we used to sit together freshman year. We're juniors now, but he's an even bigger dick than he was then, if that's possible. I look back just in time to see him grab Rafael's hand and press his fingers into the hot plastic. Raf yelps, then Anton laughs like a moron, and then all the kids in the back of the bus are scream-ing like a bunch of monkeys. I exchange eye rolls with Francesca across the aisle.

Our music appreciation teacher, Mr. Jenkins, leaps up, races down the aisle and slaps the top of Anton's seat. He tells the guys to "cut it out" in as gruff a voice as he can manage, but he sounds more like a twelve-year-old who hasn't gone through puberty yet. Anton and Raf both crack up. Mr. Jenkins turns bright red and goes back to his seat in the front. When he sits down, I think I see him wipe some sweat off the back of his neck.

I feel so sorry for Jenkins. He's probably only a few years older than Anton, and it's so obvious he's afraid of him. In fact, Mr. Jenkins seems terrified of all of us. The poor guy probably had dreams of teaching at Rutgers or whatever after he graduated from teaching school. Instead he's stuck with the dregs of Trenton Senior High, trying to get a bunch of third-generation screwups like us to give a shit about music when we can't even play instruments. We're lost causes and he knows it. I mean, I like to think Cass and I aren't, but let's face it, our futures aren't exactly golden. Cass's dad lined him up a promising job mixing cement at the asphalt plant, and I'm the grand heiress of Spin Cycle, my mom's crumbling fluff-'n'-fold empire. We'll be fine — we always are — but when Mr. Jenkins acts astonished that I haven't done my homework, I want to tell him to try going to school *and* bleaching sheets forty hours a week and see how much he feels like learning about minor scales.

I don't even know how Jenkins convinced the school to let our music class go on a field trip to Carnegie Hall. The tickets are probably in row Q of the balcony, and I guess the bus doesn't cost much, but still. The depressing part is no one except me and Cass even cares. Not about the concert, not about the city. It's basically all we've thought about since Jenkins announced the trip at the beginning of the school year, but of course it's lame to be excited about anything around here, so we keep it to ourselves.

"So, your dad lives near here, right?" Cass asks. He squeezes my arm as the bus crawls out of the Lincoln Tunnel. Light speckles the grime-filmed windows and we shield our eyes from the brightness. We stop at an intersection and a woman with impossibly tall stilettos clicks by.

"Second Avenue and 121st Street in Spanish Harlem. Not that close."

"We should grab a cab and visit him."

Ha. Hilarious. Cass knows I've only met my dad four times, and I've never even seen his apartment. Every time — at least, the times I have any memory of — was at Starbucks. Neither of us goes to Starbucks in our everyday lives, but in the warped world of me and my dad, Starbucks is our number-one hangout. I wonder what he'd do if I just showed up out of nowhere and rang his buzzer. He probably wouldn't even recognize me. I could pretend I'm a delivery girl or that I'm reading the meters. Some nobody just passing through.

"How long is this thing?" Cass asks. "A couple hours? Maybe we should sneak over to the Alvin Ailey studio instead. Watch the dancers through the windows."

"Nope. Nice try." I quit dance six months ago, and since then I've been trying to erase it from my memory. But Cass makes it impossible.

"Ugh. Fine," he says. "This new post-dance you is boring as hell. Well, we can always walk over to Times Square and people-watch at the Olive Garden, I guess. Think Jenkins will notice if we skip out?"

"I think he's got his hands full." Jenkins does his best to give Anton a menacing look. Anton responds with a for-real menacing look, then clicks his lighter and pretends to light Raf's hair on fire.

Then we're pulling up to Carnegie Hall, and everything else in the world fades away. It's weird, because it's not even that beautiful. It's just a brown brick building. Nothing special. But for some reason, just looking at it makes my chest hurt. It's like a church. Or a sturdy old oak tree with roots that stretch underground for miles in every direction. No one on the bus, not even Cass, is giving it a second look. But it's like it speaks to me.

"Actually, do you think we could just stay and watch the concert?" I ask Cass. "I don't really feel like unlimited breadsticks right now."

"I'm unable to comprehend how you could ever not feel like unlimited breadsticks, but fine," he says.

"Frank Sinatra. Your turn."

Mr. Jenkins makes us get off the bus in single file, and he hands us each a white ticket as we walk down the steps.

CARNEGIE HALL

BRIGHTON CONSERVATORY SYMPHONIC SHOWCASE
Mendelssohn Violin Concerto
in E Minor, Op. 64
Beethoven Symphony No. 3
in E Flat Major (Eroica)
September 17, 2:00 PM   PRICE $39.00

SECTION

BALC

ROW/BOX

P

SEAT

112

"Oh, my God," Cass whispers as we follow the others toward the entrance.

"What?"

"Look up."

"At what?"

He points. "That's our apartment. That's where we're going to live when we move here."

On the top floor of the building there's a row of tall, rectangular windows. I imagine going upstairs, opening the curtains and staring down at myself on the street below. My heart pounds.

"Inside Carnegie Hall?"

"That looks like an apartment, doesn't it?"

"It's probably an office."

"With red drapes? Offices have blinds."

"Since when do you know anything about drapes?"

"Since my mom's watched six hours of *House Hunters* every weekend for the last ten years."

"I bet it's, like, five thousand dollars a month."

"Who cares. We're going to be rich."

"From asphalt and dirty laundry?"

"But what about Jamie Rodriguez?"

"What about her?"

"She made it out of Trenton High School and became a star."

"She had three lines in *Zoolander 2*."

"Well, that's it, Dom. That's our place. I can feel it — I'm very intuitive. It's meant to be."

A few months ago I would have been right there with Cass, eyes full of stars. But the more I think about living in New York, the crazier it seems. How the hell are we going to get out of Trenton and all the way here? How will we make money? Who would even hire us? But I don't have the heart to say this. I'm not sure that Cass can handle the truth.

So instead I say, "It'll be amazing," and squeeze his arm. He smiles, but I glance down so I don't have to smile back.

Before we join the old people shuffling into the building, Mr. Jenkins forces all the guys to take their hats off.

"Mr. J., why does this ticket say 'Erotica'? You taking us to see porn?" Anton yells so loud an old lady with pearls turns around and glares at us.

Raf says, "Yeah, Mr. J., stop touching me against my will! Stop molesting me!"

Anton and his friends laugh like idiots and shove each other until poor Jenkins turns red and lets us go in.

We walk up a few flights of stairs that turn around and around, and just when I think they're going to go on forever, there's a carpeted area and a red curtain and an usher waving us in. We're on the fifth floor, in the top balcony. As far up as you can get without being on the ceiling. I'm dizzy, but not because of the height. I'm flooded with the same head-buzzy feeling I got when we pulled up to the building. Carnegie Hall is like a palace. The seats are a brilliant red velvet, and the walls are cream, lined with gold. On the ceiling is a bright, shimmering disk of light, with more pinpricks of light surrounding it — like the sun.

But then we sit down and it's hard to pay attention to any of it, because Anton is sitting right behind me. And the rows are so narrow his legs are practically straddling my head.

Jenkins tries to distract us from the bad seats by telling us how fantastic the sound is up here. "If we're talking acoustics, it's one of the best places to sit in Carnegie Hall," he says. "And the college students you're about to hear are the best of the best. Thousands of hopefuls from around the world audition for the chance to attend the Brighton Conservatory every year, and only a very lucky few get in. So we're in for a real treat today. Now, if you'll please take a minute to look up at this gorgeous architecture. The building was designed by William Burnet Tuthill and officially opened in 1891 ..."

Jenkins drones on and on, like he always does. But it *is* gorgeous. Maybe the most beautiful place I've ever been in my entire life. I trace the carved, glossy wood on the armrest with my fingernails.

Anton jabs his knee into my ear.

"Can you stop?" I twist around to face him, realize his crotch is, like, three inches from my head and whip my head back around again.

"What's wrong, baby girl? Last year you were begging to have my balls in your face."

His asshole friends are laughing and oohing and kicking the back of my seat. My cheeks ignite and my eyes blur. Don't let him do this to you. Don't let him do this to you. Not again.

Before I even realize what's happening, Cass stands up, turns around and raises his fist an inch from Anton's ear. "Want *this* in your face?" he asks, loud enough for the whole balcony to hear. Everyone shuts up. Anton snorts and stares at the ground. Cass sits down again.

The lights dim, and my face cools down. Cass squeezes my hand. He's the bravest person I know. He always says you have to act tough before someone else beats you to it. I wish I could wear his confidence like a blanket. Sometimes I'm so happy he's my friend it hurts.

A bunch of girls in black dresses and guys in ties and suit jackets sit down onstage with their instruments. For some reason I thought they were going to be old. Orchestras *sound* old. Like the median age is seventy-five and the players all go out to some dusty restaurant for decaf afterward. But even though they're only a few years older than Cass and me, they're sitting up straight, completely focused — not like us at all. There are some instruments I recognize, like violins and flutes and a piano and those huge violins I forget the name of that are practically the size of a person. And then there are two girls holding these tall brown tube things with thin silver mouthpieces snaking out.

And these weird circular trumpets. And these huge copper drums that look like witches' cauldrons.

An older man in a suit walks out to the front of the stage, and the audience applauds wildly. He hasn't even done anything yet, and already everyone is clapping.

Onstage, in the first row of chairs, a boy with floppy black hair stands up, holding his violin in one hand and his bow in the other. Damn, he's cute — or at least, I think he is. It's hard to tell from all the way up here. Sometimes distance can play tricks on you, and a guy you think is the hottest man alive ends up having a cowlick or a unibrow or a snaggletooth. Or worse, all three.

A guy with short blond hair, who's sitting next to the long-distance-cute boy, stands up, too. He points his bow in the air like it's an extension of his arm, and everyone starts playing the same note. At first I look at Cass like, *That's it? They're just gonna play the same thing for an hour?* But then there's silence and the blond boy sits down again.

Anton yawns loudly, and somebody shushes him. Probably Jenkins. I don't bother to turn around.

The man in the suit lifts his baton, and the musicians all lift their instruments. There's silence, silence … and then an explosion of sound so loud I flinch and Cass grabs my arm.

I'm not a gushy person. *Casablanca* never chokes me up, not even the ending. When I was a kid, I didn't cry when Bambi's mom died. I laugh in the face of that commercial with baby ducks crossing the street in tiny yellow rain boots. I roll my eyes in the greeting card aisle at the drugstore. So what happens next I'll never be able to explain.

There are at least fifty people on that stage, but through my wet eyes I can see only one: the boy with the wild black hair, playing the violin like the world's most beautiful madman.

{ 2 }

Ben

When we reach the codetta, my fingers burst into flames.

The notes on the page zoom up through my eyes and twist through my synapses and bubble in my blood and explode from my fingernails and become something bigger. Something enormous. From a flat, black-and-white grid of thirty-second notes to music. Music that's actually deserving of this place. This golden temple, where all the greatest geniuses of the last century have come to worship. Fritz Kreisler. Leonard Bernstein. Billie Holiday. And me.

And then, there's a sound. Something else.

It pinches my ear like a beesting, and my eardrum throbs and swells and puffs up to a thousand times its size. All I can hear is that note. Before he even plays it, it's hanging in the air, threatening. Then it happens, and it's everywhere, creeping across the stage, wet and sticky and stinking.

I can't let him ruin everything. If I don't stop this, we'll be just another run-of-the-mill orchestra butchering Mendelssohn on the sacred floorboards where Duke Ellington made his debut.

The second movement begins, and it's there again, waiting in the air. I can hear it — he's tentative. It's not even like he botches a phrase or his intonation is off. His bow grazes the strings too delicately, and he comes in like a shadow. He's not sure. I look up and see the landscape of quivering bows, wavering lips, twitching wrists all around me. No one is sure.

Except me. I'm sure.

Never been more sure in my life.

So my fingers ignite and slide up the strings, and I play like I always do. Like I'm in my room, playing for no one. I crack myself open and pour everything tender and passionate and vulnerable out into a pool across the stage to counteract all the nerves and terror, sweat and fear. I can't make everyone sound right, but I can turn the notes on the page into music. That's what I always do. That's what everyone counts on me to do.

And then I stop thinking.

Because once you start thinking, that's when you're really screwed.

* *

After what seems like no time at all, the audience stands and applause surrounds us. Dean Robertson puts down his baton and nods approvingly. Sweat mats his sideburns. He's obviously impressed, and it's extremely tough for students to impress him. Then he looks right at me and winks.

And everyone sees him. Amy and Kelly and, I think, Jun-Yi are staring, and I shrug and look down, because you shrug and look down when someone compliments you in public. That's what you do — you try to look small so no one hates you for being big. But I know I nailed it. Robertson knows I always nail it. Everyone knows I always nail it. I'm not being cocky or an asshole or whatever. It's just the truth.

Carter won't look me in the eye.

He knows he fucked it up.

* *

The applause lifts us into the wings, up a few twisty flights of stairs and into the greenroom backstage, filled with folding chairs and cracked-open instrument cases littered like empty oyster shells.

Claire comes in as I'm zipping my Brooks Brothers concert jacket into a garment bag. She grabs my hand.

"Ben! That was stunning," she says. "The Mendelssohn! God, you're incredible."

Her hand. It's cold and slight and fluttering. An icy moth. She lets her nerves get the best of her, and she told me she sometimes takes an Inderal before she performs. I can't take any of that stuff — won't take it, don't need it. I'm always calm when I'm on. My mom once said "eerily calm," which sounds like a serial killer, so I hate that, but I know what she means. I promise I'm not a serial killer. I'd like to take that whole story back, actually. Have it stricken from the record. Because it makes me sound insane and I promise I'm not.

But I'm always, always calm onstage.

I grip Claire's hand with both of mine and warm it up. We stand there, still and silent for a minute in the room full of noise. I know she has a crush on me. Jacob told me when we split a cab home after chamber music class. But I've noticed it, too. There's this beam of light projecting from her eyes when she looks at me. Tiny clues are everywhere. You don't have to ask girls how they feel. Just watch the light shooting out their eyes like a laser pointer and you have all the clues you need to be telepathic. I should write a book about how to become a superhero. I should write a kids' book about a violin-playing superhero who can read minds and fly through the air on the back of a giant Stradivarius. I should —

"So?" she asks.

"The last section of the first movement, right before the coda."

"What about it?"

"Carter lost it. He was so tentative you'd think he was sight-reading."

"Did Robertson notice?"

"I don't think so. The second movement was fine. The third was whatever. The first was a mess, and it was all Carter. He only gets to be the concertmaster once this semester, and he completely blew it. He's just not a leader. He almost messed up my solo on top of it. You'd think he just saw the music this morning. If anyone's going to get cut this year, it'll definitely be him. I'm calling it now."

"I didn't notice anyone else up there but you, to be honest."

Her eyes are laser-beaming all over the place, and it's making me nauseous. I let her hand go.

Claire runs over to hug Jun-Yi. I carefully pack up my violin. I'm cleaning the chin rest and wiping down the strings — sweat erodes violin strings, and my hands sweat a lot. I'm cleaning and cleaning, and I notice a dab of sweat crystallizing on the neck, so I do the whole thing over again.

Carter is staring at me.

They're all staring at me.

"I think it's clean, dude," he says, laughing.

I try to roll my eyes at Claire, but she's on the other side of the room, talking to Iman.

Once everyone else has left, Jacob and Iman and Claire and I talk about splitting a cab across town, and I make them all laugh with my old-timey cab driver impression. I try to convince them that the best idea in the world is to go get grilled cheese at Brooklyn Diner first (which is confusing, because the diner isn't in Brooklyn; it's right around the corner). Or maybe we could take a walk in Central Park, or if they want to just hang out at my place or whatever, we have every movie channel, and basically anything in the world to eat, and —

Just as we're walking out the door, Robertson calls me back. He's leaning on the edge of the piano. I tell everyone to go ahead.

The door shuts and we're alone.

"Great work today, Ben," he says.

"Thank you." I want to say more, but I keep my mouth shut. I've gotten pretty good at that at Brighton.

"You're auditioning for the Sonata Showcase?"

We have a bunch of performances at Carnegie Hall and Lincoln Center every year, but there's only one Sonata Showcase: the staggeringly important end-of-the-year concert that only twelve students in the entire school are asked to do. You and a partner (violin sonatas are always for two — usually a violinist and a pianist) get to play at Lincoln Center in front of the entire faculty. Last semester two third-years played Brahms's Violin Sonata no. 3 and got a full-page review in the *New York Times*. As a second-year student, getting into the Sonata Showcase is practically impossible. But if you do, it means universal respect from the upperclassmen. The first-years treat you like a god. Overnight you go from being lucky to be at this school to them being lucky to have you.

So I say, "Yep. Uh, yes. I'm auditioning."

"Good. Which piece?"

"*Kreutzer.* Basically because of you. Because of that thing you told me after rehearsal."

"How you're able to tap into a depth of emotion in your performance that most violinists — even at the professional level — can never attain. Love and pain all at once."

"Yeah. Well, I thought the piece would help me get more comfortable with that. Do you think it's a smart choice? I mean, I know you're not supposed to help us, but I thought especially the third movement would be —"

"With whom?"

"Claire Prescott. You know her? Of course you do. You know every-one. Anyway, we met at music camp when we were twelve, and now that we're both at Brighton we've gotten back in touch. We've been wanting to work on something together ever since —"

"The opening passage is a land mine. It needs to be fluid. Elegant."

"I'll get it."

"As I said, great work today."

"Thank you, sir."

I wait for more instruction or feedback, something, anything, but that's it. He looks at me like he's wondering why I'm still standing there. I try to access my superpowers and read his mind. There's a flicker of something, but I can't figure out what it is. Approval or indifference or a mixture of both. But he wants me to audition for the Sonata Show-case. He's *wondering* about me. He's not just a conductor — he's the dean of students, so he basically controls who succeeds here. And he's choosing me. I want to do fifty laps around the room and punch the wall and eat a thousand grilled cheese sandwiches.

Instead I run down the stairs and onto the sidewalk, through the program-clutching women and cane-carrying old men, to catch up with my friends.

* *

I forgot.

Their parents were all waiting for them. Because when you play Carnegie Hall, your parents are supposed to take off work and come and see you, even if it's in the middle of the day. No big deal. There's leftover Chinese food in the fridge and my favorite recording of the *Kreutzer* Sonata waiting for me at home.

Mom works until ten on Tuesdays, and Dad's got a board meeting with the Upper East Side Neighborhood Council about the new grocery store they're trying to put in, and Milo has his French tutor after school. So with no one waiting for me after the concert, I walk along Fifty-Seventh Street to look for a cab, running *Kreutzer* in my mind.

Don't get me wrong — my parents care and everything. When I left this morning, there was a note from Mom on the kitchen table: "Yessss! I'm so proud of you, honey! So sorry we couldn't be there this time." I'm a born-and-raised New Yorker, and I made my Carnegie Hall debut when I was eight, with the City Youth Chamber Orchestra. My parents have been to probably three hundred of my concerts in the last nine years, not to mention countless rehearsals and lessons and auditions, so it's not exactly a big deal for them anymore. I guess it shouldn't be a big deal for me, either.

My brain is too busy buzzing from the performance, anyway. I don't think I'd ever want to take drugs, but I can't imagine they'd be any better than the floating, fluorescent high I get from playing a concert and getting it right and being recognized for the billions of hours of work I do by someone who matters. Like, really matters, for my future. I've got it all mapped out: First, I need to be the best in my year. Then I need to be the best in the school. Then in the country, the world, the universe. Today it feels like I can really do it.

Then I look up and realize I'm home — Lexington Avenue and Ninety-Sixth. At least I didn't walk the wrong way, look up and find myself at the Seaport. That's happened before, as my mom loves to tell her friends: "Sometimes I think Ben's brain is just a tangle of violin strings."

"Beethoven got lost all the time and he wrote nine symphonies, nine concertos and a billion sonatas," I always shoot back.

When I get home, I head straight for the kitchen. I don't even take off my jacket. I pile a plate with lo mein and home-style tofu, brown rice and electric-green broccoli with this gloppy, delicious garlic sauce, and stick it in the microwave.

Then I text Abby and Carter and Veronica and Hadley, my grandma in Queens and Claire, even though I know she has her private lesson at seven. But no one's answering. I call Fred at Virtuoso to see if their new cases are in yet. They aren't. I make up a few more questions; do they have any chin rests with gold hardware? And do they have any gold Pirazzi E strings? Even though I know they do. But I need to keep talking to people, as many people as I can, or else the buzzy Carnegie Hall energy will stop, and I don't want it to. Not yet.

The microwave beeps. I take the plate into my room and shut the door. The smell is incredible. It's like French fries married a sesame seed and exploded all over the place. I take a giant monster bite so big it makes my jaw hurt, then run over to my laptop and hook it up to the stereo system my dad got me for my birthday.

I turn on Isaac Nadelstein and Malik Vasilyev playing *Kreutzer*, my audition piece for the Sonata Showcase. There's the tricky opening phrase Robertson was talking about. He's right — the violin starts abruptly, playing two strings at once, rolling the bow, creating the illusion of a piano chord. The bow articulation is going to be a complete bitch as the piece picks up momentum. Keeping my stamina up until the end will be rough. I have to keep my fingers light and airy and quick. If I seize up or get a cramp, the piece will fail. I listen. I chew.

I know *Kreutzer*. Most classical musicians do. Violin Sonata no. 9. Opus 47. Beethoven originally wrote it for George Bridgetower to play, but they got into a huge fight about some woman Beethoven was probably sleeping with, and at the last minute he removed the dedication and changed it to Rodolphe Kreutzer, a violinist he barely even met. It's kind of funny, because Kreutzer didn't even like Beethoven's music that much to begin with. And this piece is almost like a massive argument — it's complicated, erratic and forty-three minutes long. I heard Joshua Bell and Yuja Wang play it at Lincoln Center a few years ago, and I've listened to the Nadelstein–Vasilyev recording a billion times. I'll make it through the technique. It's about getting past it, so I can clear my brain enough to feel which notes get joy and which get pain. Which notes explode and which ones shudder. I put the first movement on Repeat. Staying in tune and in tempo with Claire will be tough when my hands are already exhausted.

Stop it. Stop thinking about technical stuff. I rub my face with my hands. I need a blank slate. I grab my violin and play the opening passage. And play. And play.

* *

"Sweetie? Ben? Ben."

"What?"

"Honey, it's almost eleven."

"And?"

"And it's pitch-black in here."

Mom's right, sort of — it's dark except for the cool-blue light from the computer screen. And the car headlights dancing in patterns on the wall. And one red pinprick of light on the stereo. So it's not exactly pitch-black, but it's too dark to see the music. I don't remember the sun setting.

Again. Again. Again.

My eyes burn when she snaps on the overhead light. I groan and rest my head in the crook of my arm until my eyes adjust. She's doing that Worried Mom thing she's so good at, busying herself by picking up crumpled tissues and fluffing my pillow and straightening the sheet music on my desk. Worrying makes her feel like a better mother.

"I'm fine," I say, hoping she'll shut the door and let me work.

I love my mom — she just drives me completely freaking crazy sometimes. She wants me to sleep eight hours a night *and* be the best violinist in the world? It doesn't work like that. Every minute you don't spend practicing, someone else is. She's a labor and delivery nurse at City Medical Center, no better or worse than any of the other nurses there. She doesn't understand.

I look up. She's still in her blue scrubs. She's been delivering babies all night. God, I feel awful for snapping at her. She's just trying to help. She's still smoothing imaginary wrinkles out of my comforter. Smoothing out my life by proxy.

"Thanks, Mom. I'm okay."

"But you didn't eat any dinner, honey."

"Yeah, I did. I had that leftover Chinese."

She points to the overflowing, untouched plate on my desk. The lo mein looks all pasty and congealed, and the broccoli is wilted and brown. Wait, I remember eating it. Didn't I eat it?

"I can make you a sandwich. There's blackberry jam from the farmers' market and —"

"I'm fine. Not hungry." I play the opening passage again.

"What are you working on?"

"*Kreutzer*. Beethoven."

"Please go to sleep soon. Don't do this tonight. Your eyes are all red, and tomorrow's your early day."

"Okay," I say, even though I have no intention of sleeping. She gives up and shuts the door. She knows I'm barely listening. There's nothing she can do.

It's quiet. I play the ache. I play the land mine.

{ 3 }

Dominique

"Rock Hudson. Your turn," I say.

"Don't change the subject."

"I don't know what you're talking about, Cass."

I yawn and turn on the TV bolted to the wall. It's 7:15 a.m. and 58 degrees, with a dew point of 52. According to the lady in the red blazer on the news, traffic is already crawling on the Jersey Turnpike. Humans shouldn't be forced to get up this early, but here we are. I have two loads to fold before Mom gets in, and Cass is drinking a giant coffee, watching me stuff clothes and detergent and color-safe bleach into the washers and not helping at all. (Not that Mom pays him.)

"You're such a baby," Cass says. "Violin Boy was right there."

"What could I even have said to him? Oh, hey, I know nothing about classical music and I've never been to Carnegie Hall before, but I just want to interrupt your very important day and whatever important stuff you have to do so I can tell you how hot you are?"

"I set the whole thing up for you! I gave you a total in, and then you cowered by the trash can until he walked away. You practically fainted."

"I didn't faint, Cass."

Okay, fine. I got that fluttery feeling in my chest and I probably did freeze for a second, but I definitely didn't cower or faint.

Here's what happened: Violin Boy walked out a side door, and Cass saw him, gasped and walked right up to him in his unapologetic Cass way. I couldn't hear much from where I was, but he basically told Violin Boy he did a great job and started making all these wild hand motions to get me to come over. But I just stood there, staring like an idiot until he thanked Cass and walked right past us. He was so close I felt a breeze from some particles of air that his arm swished toward mine. He walked right past me, through my air, making it *our* air, as he strutted down the street, violin case in hand, to the corner. Then he was one block away. And then two. And then three. And I just stood there.

Ugh. Cass is right. I'm a huge baby.

Cass sits on an upside-down laundry basket and tugs on my wrists until I give up and flop down next to him. "I've never seen you get like this over a guy," he says. "Ever. In our entire history of being best friends."

"So?"

"So, maybe you found your soul mate."

I laugh, but Cass ignores me.

"And you're acting like it's too late, like he's dead or something."

I get up to finish a seemingly endless pile of sock balls. "Well, he might as well be dead. He lives in New York, probably in some penthouse. I bet he has a pool. Heated, with, like, pink Himalayan salt in the water."

"I saw a spark. He totally glanced at you for a second. I saw, like … a little eye flutter."

"You're calling him my soul mate over an eye flutter?"

"Well, he wasn't fluttering his eyes at *me*, so at least we know he likes girls. That's something. You're halfway there."

I wince as I fold a pink thong — easily the grossest part of the job, except for maybe washing baby bibs covered in spit-up. Or old gray sheets with mysterious stains. "Fine, let's say you're right. Let's say that out of all the other girls in front of Carnegie Hall yesterday, Violin Boy noticed me. What's going to happen next? He's going to track me down in the Burg and bust into Spin Cycle and ask me out?"

"No, that's never going to happen," Cass admits. "That's why we're taking the train to New York City tomorrow to track *him* down."

I make a big deal out of pretending I don't care. But honestly? I've already considered it. Fine, I've more than considered it. For the last twelve hours the only thing I've been able to think about are the soft velvet chairs and the golden pinpricks of light on the ceiling. And the music washing over me. His music. And his hands that can make all the beauty in the world pour out of a violin. For the first time in I can't remember how long, I woke up thinking about something wonderful.

So I checked out the New Jersey Transit schedule. There are trains leaving Trenton at 3:52, 4:52 and 5:52 that could get me to the city in time to catch a glimpse of him and come back before my curfew at ten. I could tell my mom I'm staying with Cass after school to watch the basketball game and head to Deep Freeze for ice cream. It's a little over an hour from Trenton to Penn Station in New York, and it costs about $15. Plus, I'd need to take a subway to get to Lincoln Center, which is where the Brighton Conservatory is — I looked it up online. And then I could just sit on a bench or something and wait until he gets out of class and then, as he's about to walk away, tap him on the shoulder and tell him I'm sorry for bothering him, but I just want to say how great he was in the concert. I don't have anything planned out after that.

Cass goes into this whole speech about how I'll never know if he's the one for me unless I track him down and find out for myself. I shake my head and look down until my hair falls in my eyes and tell him, "No way. That's so stupid."

But I've already decided.

I'm going.

* *

But here's the thing that sucks: money. It's not like I have $15 and another $5 for the subway just lying around. That's our food budget for the whole week. I'm almost eighteen, and I don't even have a bank account. Mom's always made sure we live in an apartment on a safe street no matter what, but sometimes that means eating rice and beans three days in a row or taking the laundry no one picks up to the thrift store to sell. After a bag of clothes stays unclaimed for thirty days we can do whatever we want with it, and it happens more often than you'd think. You'd figure people, especially in this neighborhood, would want to pick up their laundry, but sometimes they just disappear. Who knows what happens to them. They get arrested or evicted and have to move. I hate to think about it, but maybe they die. Or maybe they're so messed up they forget they dropped off their clothes in the first place.

So every couple of months, Mom scours Spin Cycle and the apartment for things we can sell or trade in. Sometimes she'll take a few extra shifts at the Dollar Plenty, where she used to work before she bought the laundromat. Or she'll make a deal with Ronaldo, the super, to do odd jobs around our apartment building, like paint the hallway or pick up trash on the front steps. He won't give us cash, but he'll sometimes let us pay late, or even give us a break in our rent. We're lucky. Mom moved here with my dad right before I was born, so everyone knows us and Ronaldo knows we're good for the rent. Sometimes that's all that keeps us afloat from month to month: faith that we're good for it. And we are, eventually.

Sometimes I wonder if Mom should just give up — sell the laundromat and go back to the Dollar Plenty full-time, even though she's invested so much money in her business. She keeps hoping sales are going to pick up, that miraculously the town will turn around and there will be a bunch of new families moving in. We wait and hope, and nothing changes.

Anyway, $20 isn't easy to come by.

* *

Mom comes in at 7:45 with a half-eaten apple in one hand and a bag full of delicates from Mrs. Fisher in the other. She picks up Mrs. Fisher's things once a week, no charge — Mrs. Fisher is eighty-six and lives around the corner in a six-floor walk-up. My mom doesn't want her climbing the stairs and breaking a hip, which I think is so sweet of Mom. She's always doing nice stuff like that for everyone in the neighborhood. She's been teaching me kindness by example since I was a baby, but I'm still not as good at it as she is.

"Sorry I'm late," she says, giving both me and Cass kisses. Cass's mom has issues. She's not really much of a parent to him. So my mom knows it means a lot to him when she treats Cass like he's a member of our family. Sometimes I wonder if he only hangs out with me in the mornings because it's one less hour of the day he has to spend in his apartment, with the dirty clothes in the hallway and the leak in the living room.

"You guys better get out of here," Mom says, "I heard the first bell on the way over. Oh, Dom, can you pick up a jug of white vinegar on the way home? The change machine is looking pretty cruddy."

"Sure. Anything else?"

"Yeah, there's frozen spinach on sale at C-Town. Can you pick up three packages?"

"Sure."

"And try to get Sal on the register — he gives double coupons if you ask."

"I know."

Cass looks at me expectantly. I can tell he wants me to ask my mom about tomorrow night. I roll my eyes and grab my backpack.

"Oh, um, Mom?"

"What?"

"I'll get a receipt," I say under my breath, and try to bolt out the door, but Cass is too quick for me. He grabs my elbow and puts his arm around my shoulder so I can't escape.

"Also, Ms. Hall, do you think Dom could come with me, Jasmine and Francesca to the basketball game tomorrow after school? They're playing Hopewell."

"You have study hall tomorrow after music?" she asks me.

"Yeah."

"So you'll get all your homework done then?"

"Yeah, definitely."

"Do you have any tests?"

"No, just the geometry pop quiz from yesterday."

"And you're caught up on chores? You'll vacuum on Saturday?"

"Yeah."

"Okay," she says at last, then grabs Mrs. Fisher's delicates and loads them into the washing machine in the corner.

And that's it. I'm going to New York City to track down Violin Boy tomorrow. Easiest thing in the world.

Cass and I get to school just as the last bell rings.

"Don't stress about the train," Cass says before we head in opposite directions to homeroom. "My grandma gave me some birthday money, and there's nothing I'd rather spend it on than the promise of true love." He bats his eyes.

"You're ridiculous," I say, and shove him, but I can't stop smiling. Today there's a brightness in my life. A glow around the edges I've never felt before. And now that I feel it I can't let it go away. I go through six classes and a trip to C-Town, then back to the store to help Mom clean and close, with a big stupid grin on my face. Maybe I'll wait at Lincoln Center for three hours and Violin Boy won't even come. Maybe he'll be sick tomorrow. Maybe he's on vacation. Maybe he only has class until three on Thursdays. Maybe he has a doctor's appointment or another concert, or he's going to meet his family for lunch, or he has a friend's recital across town or another music lesson somewhere else entirely, in Harlem or Queens or Park Slope.

Or maybe he'll be there.

{ 4 }

Ben

"Let's take it again from the B section. And try it this time with a little bit more … I don't know. Agony."

Yaz waves his hand at us indiscriminately. I wish teachers would be more specific.

Our orchestra repertoire class (or orchestra rep, for short) is supposed to be a chance for Yaz's private students to all get together and dissect symphonies, but today I'm the only one paying attention. The others are all sitting up with their backs straight, but I can see it in their eyes. They're exhausted. They were up too late, or they had an early class, or playing eight-plus hours a day has finally started catching up with them. Thankfully Carter has a different private teacher, so at least I don't have to hear him ruining Paganini.

Yaz stops us. "Wait, Ben, what are you doing?"

"What do you mean?"

"Your fingering."

"I thought I'd go up the string instead of crossing."

"Why? It doesn't change the sound of the phrase and it's twice as difficult."

Because I can.

"Why not?" I smile.

"Again from B, please, and we'll go on to the end of the movement. Crossing is fine — no need to get fancy."

He shakes his head at me, but I see him smirking behind his music stand.

Yaz is a former Sydney Symphony Orchestra first chair, and I've been going to his apartment for lessons since I was eight. My parents picked him because he teaches at Brighton. He rarely takes on students so young, so I knew I had a good chance, but there was still no guarantee I'd get into the conservatory. My audition had to be perfect. And it was. Because I've been going to him forever, he never lets me get away with anything — even though playing up the string would be way more exciting than a boring cross, and he knows it.

When we make it to the end, Yaz calls a twenty-minute break, but I don't want to stop. I want to go over the B section a dozen more times just to make sure it's ingrained. But then I see Yaz reviewing the second ending with Lilly, and I realize that's more important — it could take her days to master — so I leave them alone and go outside. At least I can practice my fingering.

I cut across the Lincoln Center campus — a majestic, cream-colored sprawl of theaters, opera houses and concert halls that takes up three entire city blocks. It's mostly empty today, except for a few people sitting on benches and eating late lunches, plastic clamshells resting in their laps. And the tourists. Always the tourists, wearing fleece jackets and giant backpacks and taking photos of everything with their phones, like they can't just download a way better photo of the Metropolitan Opera House online. But today even the guy in the Montana State hat who is balancing on top of a ledge and trying to snap a photo of a squirrel isn't bothering me. Everything in my life has clicked into place. I've always known I have what it takes to be the best violinist at Brighton. And now everyone else knows it, too. All I have to do is get *Kreutzer* right, and I'll be unstoppable. Then all the millions of hours alone in my room will have been worth it.

It's cold and the sun's setting, casting a blinding glare on the windows of Avery Fisher Hall. I walk over to the fountain, my favorite people-watching spot, and lean against the stone ledge to try to soak up some of the warmth. My mission isn't too successful, because it's a little windy, and droplets of water from the fountain keep splashing the back of my neck. I'm about to get up and go back to class, when there's a subway map in my face.

And a stunning girl standing in front of me, holding the map with both hands.

"Hey, can you help me find the A train?" she asks.

It's weird she's holding an actual paper map. There are a million subway apps. This map is torn and soft like it's been folded up and carried around inside thousands of pockets.

"How Duke Ellington of you," I say, then immediately realize this girl probably knows nothing about jazz. For all I know, she thinks Duke Ellington is the newest guy on *The Bachelor*. For all I know, she's just another tourist, heading uptown to find more squirrels to photograph.

"I'm more of a Frank Sinatra girl, but if he can help me get to Washington Square, sure."

Wait. Frank Sinatra? Who *is* this girl? I give her a glance up and down but pretend to cough so she won't notice. She definitely doesn't go to Brighton. No way. She has thick, curly hair, springing out in all directions and this casual, cool look that all the girls at Brighton try to do but none even come close to pulling off. Kids at conservatories aren't casual. This girl is relaxed, not trying too hard. NYU, maybe?

"Over there," I tell her, pointing toward the Apple store. "Just go down the steps and straight down, then turn right at Seventy-Second and you'll see the station a few blocks over. Just don't cross Seventy-Second, that's for uptown. Stay on this side of the street, and then look out for a green lamppost — although I don't know if it would even be considered a lamppost, because I've never seen it lit up. It's more of a globe." I'm doing my usual talking-too-much thing and have to will myself to stop. Nothing good ever comes from adding a second sentence. Or a third. Or a fourth.

"Thanks," she says, and smiles.

She has these huge white teeth — and one of them, the left eyetooth, is twisted in the wrong direction, kind of like her hair. She's wearing tight jeans and you can tell she's got a great, curvy body and a really nice butt, but then she has a billowy, too-big purple T-shirt on that somehow looks amazing, anyway. She's not trim and tiny and neat like Claire or Jun-Yi or the other classical-music clones at school. She's flowy and messy and jumbled, but in this totally beautiful way. Like jazz.

"Were you seeing a concert?" I ask. Just to keep the conversation going.

"Huh?"

"The recital at Avery Fisher or something?"

"Me?"

Like there's anyone else I could be talking to.

"No, but I'd love to see something here one day," she says.

"So you're just killing time after class?"

"Uh, yeah, I don't —"

"Let me guess. NYU."

She smiles. "Yeah. Yes."

"And you think Frank Sinatra was a better performer than Duke Ellington?"

"No, I just don't know that much about jazz. Old movie musicals are more my thing. Like *Singin' in the Rain* and *West Side Story*."

"And *Porgy and Bess*? Well, I guess it's technically an opera, but it was on Broadway and was written by Gershwin, so whatever. Anyway, there's a song in it — 'Summertime.'"

Her eyes glow. "I know 'Summertime.'"

"Well, Frank Sinatra covered it, but so did Billie Holiday, who was, hands down, the greatest female jazz singer of all time. She also sang 'I Loves You, Porgy.' Jazz and Broadway aren't that different."

"Like how Louis Armstrong sang 'Hello, Dolly.'"

Oh. My. God. This girl knows Louis Armstrong.

"Exactly. And John Coltrane covered 'My Favorite Things.'"

"From *The Sound of Music*, right?"

"You know more about jazz than you think."

She grins this big, wide, earth-moving smile, and I realize I'm grinning, too. This is the first time I've felt relaxed in I don't know how long. When I look at her — whoever she is — I don't think about school or competitions or codas or strings. She's all I can see, for miles and miles and miles.

She lifts her hand and tucks her hair behind her ear. She misses a stray piece and I want — God, more than anything — I want to tuck it behind her ear for her. I don't know where this comes from or why I want to do it, but it feels like the most important thing in the world at this particular second. She's perfectly capable of tucking her hair behind her own ear, I don't know why she would ever need my help. I don't know where I get off thinking I can go around just tucking girls' hair behind their ears for them. But then I realize my hand is reaching out, completely against my will, and getting ready to do it, and — oh, my God, don't do it, don't do it, she's going to think you're a creep — and I jam my hand in my pocket, even though there's nothing in there.

And now she's going to wonder why I just stuck my hand in my pocket. Maybe I should offer her some gum. Crap, I have no gum. Maybe I should offer her some anyway and hope she says no. Or I could pull this tissue out of my pocket and blow my nose — ugh, no, no girl wants to see you blowing your nose; just take your hand out of your pocket, you idiot.

"Well, I should go," she says.

And I realize we've been standing in complete silence for thirty seconds. Then she's looking down at the ground and flushing all red again and mumbling a thank you in the softest piccolo voice and walking the wrong way down the steps.

"Hey," I yell after her. "Other side."

She laughs at herself and waves, then turns and walks in the right direction. "Take the 'A' Train" blares in my head and I tap out the fingering on the fountain ledge.

* *

When I get home, there's a note on the kitchen table from Mom telling me to order takeout ("something healthy, please — not Brooklyn Diner") for me and Milo. He should be getting home from tennis any minute. Mom and Dad are having their monthly "Let's Keep Our Marriage Alive" Date Night, which has seemed to work for them so far, but then again, I don't exactly ask questions about whether they're happy with each other.

They always go someplace really nice where it takes weeks to get a reservation. The kind of place that has a tasting menu with dessert included, but you're way too stuffed for your tiramisu or whatever, so you take it home in a paper box with the name of the restaurant embossed in gold on the lid. When we were younger, Milo and I used to fight over who'd get to eat it the next day. Now I just let him have it.

I have more important things to do.

* *

I lose hours when I'm in my room. Even with the metronome counting each second I still couldn't tell you if I've been in my room for five minutes or five hours. When Milo gets home, he knocks on my door quietly. He knows not to bother me when I'm practicing, so I ignore him. But the knocking gets louder and more insistent, until I finally set my violin down on my bed, fling the door open and yell, "What?" He looks pissed off and I feel bad for yelling, and then I'm trying to save face by asking him how tennis practice was and did he win any matches, like pretending to be interested for thirty seconds will fix anything. Milo sees right through me.

"I was just going to ask what you want for dinner," he says. "Mom told me I had to make you eat something. Like you're six and I'm babysitting."

"I'm fine," I say, and grab the violin. "I ate lunch late." I tune him out and inject tension into *Kreutzer*. Milo's a freshman in high school, so technically no, he shouldn't have to worry about his older brother. But if it were up to him, we'd be sitting on the couch watching old *Seinfeld* reruns together and stuffing ourselves with Doritos. I can't let myself do that, not even for a second. Because if you do that for one night, that's a night another violinist will spend practicing. Another violinist I'll be up against someday.

Milo puts his hand on my strings. "I'm ordering sushi," he says.

"That's fine," I say, pulling away.

He walks out and shuts the door.

Alone again, and time unravels.

* *

Claire sends me a text around eleven: *Run through Kreutzer tomorrow after theory?*

I bet she's getting ready for bed — we have class at eight tomorrow. I'm still practicing the opening passage.

Cool, I write back. *Will reserve practice room after my private lesson.*

Cool, she writes. *Wear that shirt with the green stripes. Brings out your eyes.*

I don't respond, but I smile.

I keep smiling through my string crossings, and for some reason they sound more effortless. Like somehow my fingers know I'm smiling and they transfer the energy to the violin. It's weird, but it works.

Again. Again. Again.

"Honey ..."

Mom. Of course it's Mom. Who else would it be?

"Yeah?"

"What are you playing? Sounds like Duke Ellington."

"No, it's a sonata."

"Weren't you just playing that 'Take the "A" Train' song? That's what it sounded like."

"Oh, right." That's weird. I guess I was. My mind drifts back to the subway girl with the big hair and the tight jeans and the too-loose shirt.

"Okay, honey, time for bed. It's after midnight."

"Sorry," I say. "Lost track of time."

She says nothing but lays a packet of printed computer paper, stapled in the corner, in my lap. It's a *New York Times* article about the importance of sleep for people they're calling "Super Achievers." I groan and let it slide to the floor.

"I'm fine," I say. "I have to get this right. Do you want me to be first violin at the New York Phil, or do you want me to work in middle management at an office?"

Without a word she sets a cup of tea and a piece of toast with peanut butter next to me on the bed. She shuts the door with a click before I can say thank you.

I mean to drink the tea, but then it stops seeming important.

{ 5 }

Dominique

I can't go home now.

Maybe I'll just walk this noisy, magnificent city up and down, from the tip of the Bronx to the end of the Brooklyn Bridge, over and over, forever. I'll never need to eat or sleep again. Not with the city sustaining me.

The A train leads me to a neighborhood I've never seen before. The streets in the West Village have given up on the grid system that the rest of the city follows. Instead the streets collide with one another. Please let me get lost here. Let me lose my way and have to wander this maze a little longer.

It's getting dark, but not the way it does in Trenton. The city isn't emptying out. The sidewalks are full of people out on dates and running errands after work and hanging out by the subway station and hailing cabs on the corner and eating folded pizza on paper plates. I pass a movie theater — the marquee blazes with old round lightbulbs. It's playing a bunch of art movies I've never heard of. And a midnight showing of *Singin' in the Rain* — which, of course, I have.

I imagine my own story: It's quarter to twelve, and Violin Boy is standing by the box office, waiting for me. When he sees me, he smiles exactly the way he did when I told him I knew Louis Armstrong. His eyes crinkle, so blue they're almost black. He pulls two tickets out of his pocket, and we go in. He holds my hand the whole time and puts his arm around me when Don Lockwood gives Kathy Selden the sweetest of goodnight kisses in the rain. (Right before the most genius dance number of all time, the title number, filmed when Gene Kelly was deliriously sick with a 103-degree fever. But he was such a pro you'd never even know.)

After the movie, still holding hands, we turn the corner onto a quiet side street, illuminated with twinkling streetlamps and lined with cobblestone. We pass the brick brownstones with wrought-iron gates and blooming flower boxes in every window. A cab slows down and drops someone off across the street, then flips its Off Duty light on and drives away. An old couple on an evening stroll passes us and smiles. Then we walk up the steps to the brownstone that's ours, and he opens the door. We close it behind us, shutting off the rest of the world, until morning.

I'd never really noticed before, but walking in New York City is like wearing an invisibility cloak. I can dream and explore, and no one bothers me. Not like at home, where everyone's constantly up in your business. How you have to act tough before someone else beats you to it, like Cass always says. All I can think of is how right everything feels. I know I belong here.

Now that I know where his classes are, I have to spend more time at Lincoln Center to increase the chances I'll run into Violin Boy again. Drink in another glimpse of his wild black hair. Devour the way his hand grips the fountain with its close-clipped nails and pale skin. Not *too* pale. Just white and smooth and cool, like a bowl of melted French vanilla ice cream.

I have no idea why he thinks I go to NYU. I couldn't make up a lie that amazing in a million years. I guess the dorms are near the West Fourth Street subway station, so he just assumed. Does he think I could be in college? I can't believe he thinks I seem smart enough — or rich enough — to go to a school like NYU.

The funny thing is, I always dreamed of going to NYU, back when I thought I might be a dancer. When I was little, I'd spend hours in the living room every weekend learning routines from old musicals. Mom put me in dance lessons — jazz and tap and ballet — at the community center. Renee, my jazz teacher, had studied dance at NYU and said she might be able to write me a recommendation letter if I wanted. But then Mom bought the laundromat and started needing me to work on the weekends, and money started getting tighter, and I realized NYU was a dream that people like me don't get to have. So I quit. I told Mom I got sick of it. That I decided I didn't want to be a dancer after all. That the classes were boring. But I think she knows the real reason.

Anyway.

I have to tell him the truth the next time I see him. If there is a next time. I'll go back to the city and meet him by the fountain again and tell him he misunderstood. But wait. If he thinks I go to school here, I have an excuse to be hanging around all the time. I could pretend I'm doing research for class at Lincoln Center. I think I saw a library there. I could see him every day. Okay, it's ridiculous. There's no way I could realistically take the train into the city every night after school. But right now, it sounds like the best idea I've ever had.

* *

It's too late to walk home from the train station. My mom's told me a billion times: "If you have to be out after ten, make sure Cass is with you." I briefly consider calling him when the train pulls in — he's always said he'll walk over and get me wherever I am, no matter what time. But I don't. Instead I grip my pepper spray in my jacket pocket and walk as fast as I can.

On my twelfth birthday, Mom bought me the tiny silver tube of pepper spray on a keychain. I've had to use it two-and-a-half times.

The first time: In seventh grade I was walking home from tap class and a drug addict (or at least, he looked like he was) with greasy, stringy hair threw a beer bottle at me. It shattered on the sidewalk, and glass shards rained onto my shoes.

The second time: In eighth grade a man in a gray hooded sweatshirt put his hands in the back pockets of my shorts and pressed himself against me. I screamed and he ran away before I could see his face. Mom called 911 when I got home, but I'm not sure they ever did anything. The cops have more important things to worry about.

The almost-third time: Last year Anton flashed me his cousin's gun, in a holster under his shirt. Not to hurt me or anything. Just to show me he could protect me. Who knows whether his cousin let him borrow it or he took it without asking, but either way he shouldn't have had it. I held the spray to his face, right near his eye, and he put the gun back inside his shirt. I never told anyone, not even Cass. That's the type of thing a person could go to jail for, and I wouldn't wish that on anybody. Not even Anton the Asshole. Not when he's so close to graduating — the one thing no one ever expected him to do. I still find myself smiling when he passes a pop quiz. I don't want him to be stuck in high school, torturing Jenkins forever.

Home safe — almost. Before I unlock the door to our building, I peek through the tiny window just to make sure no one's hiding in the entryway.

I run up the three flights and put my key in our door. Mom's asleep on the couch, so I use my phone as a light and try to be quiet. There's only one bedroom, and we're supposed to take turns sleeping in the bed. I wash my face, brush my teeth and change into my mom's big gray T-shirt. I jump high in the air and fall backward onto the bed. My body makes a satisfying thud on the mattress.

I am electric.

* *

The next morning Cass corners me by the dryers.

"Why didn't you call me back? What happened?"

"There's nothing to tell. I saw him."

"You what?" Cass collapses on the ground and pretends to faint.

"That floor hasn't been mopped in a week."

He jumps up. "Ew. So what's his name?"

"Still don't know."

"What do you mean, you don't know? I even typed 'violinist Brighton dark hair' into my phone yesterday to see if something would come up. Don't tell me you didn't check Facebook or anything."

"I guess I didn't think about it." Oh, I'd thought about it. I'd searched for hours.

"Okay, Miss Innocent, you're driving me nuts. What happened?"

"There's just not much to tell. I saw him, he helped me with subway directions, and that was it."

"Are you kidding? That's huge! He knows who you are now. That's the first step — now you have to go back tomorrow so he remembers you."

"No, I need to help my mom tomorrow, especially because she gave me last night off. I'll go next week or something."

"By next week he'll forget you. You'll have to start all over. Time is of the essence, Dom, trust me. I've seen *Casablanca* forty-seven times. This is my field of expertise. I don't question you about, like, fabric softener."

"When have I ever said anything about fabric softener?"

"It's just a hypothetical. Look, tomorrow is imperative to the whole plan."

"Stop getting your hopes up. Nothing's going to happen." Really, I want Cass to stop getting *my* hopes up. Because if I go back and visit Violin Boy and nothing happens, I'm not sure I can take the disappointment.

Cass turns an empty laundry basket upside down and stands on top of it. Oh, God, he's about to make a speech.

He clears his throat.

"Dominique Angelica Hall. When you were sick with the flu last year and I brought over *Breakfast at Tiffany's*, do you think we were watching that for fun? You think I sat there sobbing through 'Moon River' for the seventeenth time for my own benefit? No — that movie has taught me one of the most important lessons of my life, and it's that in New York City you can be absolutely anyone you want to be. You don't need a lot of money or status to be glamorous and captivating and magical. So get your gorgeous, captivating, magical butt on that train, track down Violin Boy and never look back."

Okay, fine. It was a pretty good speech.

* *

Who even does this?

Who spends two hours and $20 traveling to New York City to stand outside some random building, hoping for a two-second glimpse of someone she doesn't even know?

You know who does this? A stalker.

He's going to think I'm a total freak. He's going to call the cops and get a restraining order against me, and I'm going to end up on one of those detective shows where they try to figure out what the weirdo's motive was. The Music Conservatory Creeper. They're going to have a police sketch of me and everything.

Mom thinks I'm studying with Cass. She always lets me off if she thinks I'm doing homework. She's a really fast folder and great at customer service and is totally capable of closing up the store by herself, but I hate to think of her getting lonely. Especially because we haven't had as many customers the last few months. I suspect that people are starting to go to the nicer twenty-four-hour chain off Route 1 with the free dryers. But I don't tell Mom that. I just keep saying we're in a lull and it's a tough season because people dry their clothes on the line outside. I try to believe it, too.

So I'm feeling like a completely terrible daughter. Instead of helping my mom like I should be, I'm spending Cass's money and some of my birthday cash from my dad. (Every year, about three weeks after my birthday, he sends a card with a $50 bill in it, and only one word written inside: Reg. Not even Dad — just Reg. Like we're poker buddies or something.) And I'm standing outside waiting for some guy I don't even know, not so I can introduce myself but so I can gawk at him as he walks across the street.

I wonder if I'll have a roommate in jail, or if they sentence stalkers to solitary confinement.

At least this time I'm armed with supplies: A few Fosse books I got out of the Trenton Public Library (I've decided that I'm a dance major at NYU — it's something I actually know something about). My backpack. And a half-empty plastic water bottle like I just came from a dance class. I'm wearing black stretchy leggings and a tank top with a hot-pink sports bra. It's an outfit I used to wear to dance all the time, but for the last few months it's been crumpled up in the back of my drawer.

Who even does this?

I can't breathe. I didn't realize I'd be this nervous. I sling my backpack on one shoulder, then both, then one shoulder again, then I hold it in my hand. The insides of my wrists are getting sweaty and

I feel like I have to pee, and my foot keeps tapping and twitching, and what if he doesn't have class in this building today? Or worse, what if he sees me and immediately realizes I'm waiting for him?

But none of that happens. Something worse does.

Brighton Conservatory's big glass front door opens and there he is. Violin Boy, with a messenger bag slung over his shoulder and his violin case under his arm. He's with a girl.

She has smooth red hair that stops at her chin and curls under just slightly, like she spent an hour blow-drying it but wants to trick everyone into thinking it's natural.

She has pink pearl earrings and lavender manicured nails and she's wearing a white-collared shirtdress with a thin leather belt at the waist and a pale-pink cardigan. She's effortlessly, breezily, impossibly beautiful.

And she's holding his hand.

* *

They cross on the flashing red sign, so I run to catch up before the light changes. I need to find out if she's his girlfriend. If she is, this whole thing is pointless. A woman wearing yoga pants and pushing a stroller, an older man with a hunched back, and a spiky-haired preschooler with his nanny are all crossing with me, so I try to blend in. They turn onto Central Park West, and I follow.

We pass Sixty-Fifth Street, Sixty-Sixth Street, Sixty-Seventh, Sixty-Eighth, Sixty-Ninth. At some point Violin Boy and the breezy girl drop hands, but they're still laughing. Her wrists are so thin and delicate. I bet she goes on ten-day detoxes where she eats nothing but room temperature vegetable broth. I bet she loves cucumber slices with hummus — not because they're good for you but because she likes the taste. She probably eats 1,200 calories a day — no more, no less. She's the complete epitome of everything I could never be.

I glance down at my leggings, which are worn out at the knees. The hem around the right ankle is starting to unravel. They're the best pair I own.

Seventy-First Street, Seventy-Second, Seventy-Third. I'm trying to stay at least half a block behind them, but they keep slowing down. I'm starting to get that sick, twisty knot in my chest, and I know I should turn around and go back in the other direction. I'm not sure where the nearest subway station is, but I know I'm at least thirty blocks from the train I need to take home. And there's no way I can afford a cab. But even though it's killing me to see him hold hands with another girl, I can't bring myself to leave. Standing outside his life and looking in is better than not being there at all. And I need to know who she is.

The girl puts her hand on his back and they both laugh. I have to know the end of the story. Violin Boy moves the fingers of his left hand in a beautiful frenzy, grasping for strings that aren't there. I wonder what song he's playing. She gives him another nudge and tries to take his hand, but he's too distracted. He's too busy playing the stone wall that separates the street from the park.

Then, I'm not sure why, he turns around.

{ 6 }

Ben

Claire keeps going on and on about her teacher Marie. Her last private lesson was crappy and she's nervous Marie won't push her enough to help her nail *Kreutzer*. Claire hasn't had a standout moment at Brighton yet, and the rest of the faculty barely know who she is. So she's wondering if Marie is the right teacher to get her noticed. I want to tell her she should have thought about that before spending ten years studying with Marie and following her here, but of course I don't say that. I would never say that. Claire is panicking and we both know it. I wish she'd realize that every ounce of energy she wastes on worrying about the piece she could actually spend *learning* the piece. That's the difference between people who succeed and people who fail — people who don't make it get bogged down by logistics; the select few who succeed transcend it all.

"How many hours a night are you practicing?" Claire asks as we walk toward the park. "I'm aiming for four after class and it's just killing me. Last night I fell asleep on the keys."

I practice until the notes on the page become music. Time is meaningless. But I'll sound like a complete asshole if I say that. Don't say that. Don't say that.

"I don't know — three hours a night or something," I say instead.

"Three, okay, I think I can handle three. I have to practice smarter. It's just, after class all day, the only thing I want to do is eat takeout and fall asleep in front of the TV, you know?"

"Yeah, I know. It's all about balance," I say, even though I don't and it isn't. But sometimes I think that thing astounding musicians have — the ability to take a two-dimensional page and make the notes bloom and roar — is something you can't teach. Either it's there or it isn't. If she's even thinking about the number of hours, I'm not sure there's anything I can say to help her. Did Beethoven ever think about stuff like this? Great music can't be quantified or measured. It's infinite.

I'm probably being too hard on Claire. She got into Brighton; that's a pretty big deal in itself. Thousands of pianists audition every year and she's one of the ten who got in. But even at the best music school on earth you look around and realize that most people will never be extraordinary. They're just human.

Well, except one guy. This morning we rode the elevator with Isaac Nadelstein, one of the greatest violinists in the history of the world. He teaches workshops and master classes here when he isn't touring. I held my breath the whole time, which was probably a good idea, because it kept me from talking.

But now I regret not saying hello. He's an alumnus of the school and he has his own music program here, so I'm sure I'll run into him again, and I need to come up with the perfect thing to say. I'm here because of you? Too suck-uppy. You're an inspiration to all of us? Too cheesy. I'm in awe of you and I want to name all my future kids after you, even the girls? Too over the top.

I've completely stopped paying attention to Claire, but when I enter reality again, it turns out I haven't missed much. She's still talking about Marie, and whether I think she should say something to her. If it were me, would I say something to Yaz? I'm not sure, I tell her, I think it would depend on the situation. She keeps holding my hand and petting me and putting her arm on my shirt — all these weird things she doesn't usually do, and to be honest, I'm not even sure why she's doing them.

Don't get me wrong — I like it. I mean, what guy doesn't like a hot girl touching his arms and everything? But there's this weird thing with Claire where I can't tell if she's being nice to me because she wants something, or because she actually likes me. She's never gotten a solo at school before. She's auditioned, but the faculty didn't think she was ready. So if she auditions with someone who's played a solo at Carnegie Hall — me — I wonder if she's thinking it will increase her chances of getting into the Sonata Showcase in the spring. Then Robertson and the rest of the faculty will finally notice her and she'll be on track to get solos of her own and do competitions next semester. Maybe that's why she's been all over me recently. Or maybe she really does have a crush on me, like Jacob said. Either way, her attention makes me tingly and completely confused.

We're walking near Central Park, and I don't know why, but I suddenly wish I was walking alone. She's just going on and on. I don't want to hold her hand anymore, so I drop it.

I need to go home.

Then I look behind me to see if I can hail an oncoming cab, and there she is. The girl from NYU with the curly hair and the loose shirt and the twisted tooth. My chest floods with that same calmness I felt the first time I saw her by the fountain.

"Hey, A Train!" I yell, before I realize what I'm doing.

At first she doesn't do anything. She freezes, like I've caught her shoplifting. Then she turns and looks over her shoulder, like I couldn't possibly be talking to her.

Claire grabs my hand again.

I don't want A Train to leave.

But she takes off running.

Down the steps and into the park and gone.

I'm left with nothing but Claire's hand. A hand I never even meant to hold.

* *

I put in my earbuds and turn up *Kreutzer*. It's okay that I'm not practicing, because at least I'm listening. It's good to take a night off and rest my hands once in a while. My left arm has been feeling a little out of whack the last few days, anyway. If my mom knew, she'd tell me I was exhausting myself. She doesn't know my arm's been bugging me, and she doesn't know I haven't been sleeping so great. Well, I took a long nap on Wednesday, but that's only because I was seeing stars when I tried to play the first movement. When I woke up, I was invincible again.

My cab driver blows through the light at Eighth Street, and I tell him he can stop right at Washington Square Park. NYU doesn't have a campus, but the park is kind of like their quad. She'll have to be coming or going from some class eventually. I wonder if her dorm is one of these buildings with all the kids hanging out in front of them, or if she lives way off campus. A bunch of slacker-looking guys are sitting out on the front steps, smoking in these bright hats and tank tops, even though it's starting to get cold. God, what if she smokes? I hope she doesn't smoke.

The second movement begins in my ears, and like a reflex, I sit down on a bench and play it in my mind. Listening is as important as actually practicing, I remind myself, and try to ignore my guilt. I'm seventeen. I deserve to have some semblance of a life. Isaac Nadelstein somehow has time to be one of the greatest violinists in the world, teach, tour and have five kids. If he can do that, I can sit on a bench for twenty minutes and look for A Train without feeling like a total waste of life.

But that nagging feeling keeps coming, so I turn up *Kreutzer* until it's too loud to focus on anything else. I practice my fingering to keep that other noise out of my brain.

Twenty minutes turns into thirty, and the sun sets and it's dark, and even the smoking kids decide to go inside, probably to the dining hall to stuff their faces with fries and self-serve frozen yogurt. I wonder what their nights are like. I doubt they have much homework, or if anyone even cares whether they show up to their humanities lectures or whatever. Sometimes I get jealous when I think about how much freedom normal kids have. I wonder if I could be happy with a life like that. They're probably going in to catch up on some TV show they're obsessed with, or sit around and drink smuggled-in beer and play Kings Cup. We tried to play it at Jun-Yi's place one time when her parents were gone, and the whole game ended up with us arguing about the first movement of Beethoven's *Pastoral*. I think it's one of the lamest, most predictable movements in all classical music, and Jun-Yi and Claire think it's pretty. Ugh.

Now, in the darkness, there's only a man walking a dog, and an older woman dozing on a bench across the park.

And me.

And no curly-haired girl.

I check my phone and there are fourteen texts from Mom.

* *

"All I ask is that you call me," Mom says, in the middle of a rant before I even open the front door. "Keep me in the loop, let me know where you're going. That's really the only rule I have, Ben. You can go to concerts and shows and art exhibits with your friends whenever you want, you don't have a curfew … You have it a lot better than most kids, you realize that?"

"You're right," I say, knowing I'll never win this one. "I lost track of time. I'm sorry."

"You're always losing track of time. Milo is three years younger than you. How does he manage to get home on time? Why are you the one I'm always having to worry about?"

When Mom gets upset, the first thing she does is compare her kids. Biggest parenting mistake in the book, but she does it every time. "I'm sorry, I'm sorry, I'm sorry," I repeat, trying to look pitiful, until she has no choice but to stop. The central air kicks in. She glances up at the vent and sighs. I give her a kiss on the cheek and say it one more time: "I'm sorry. I don't know what I was thinking."

"I'd like to be inside your mind for a day, just to see what it's like," she says. She sounds sad and far away, like she's already lost me. I give her a hug and try to infuse some reassurance and love into it, but I don't think it works.

"Don't make me worry," she says.

And then she tries to force a bunch of food on me. I take some toast and a glass of orange juice to my room to make her happy. She's always trying to get me to eat these huge, heavy meals, but all I can handle are snacks right now. I get too slow, too tired when I eat too much, and you can hear it when I play.

I set my violin case on my bed and head right for the computer. I go to the NYU website and find a roster of incoming students. There are 5,867 freshmen — 2,986 female — and they're all listed alphabetically. I type the first name on the list, Veronica Aarons, into Google Images.

Up comes a red-haired girl with straight teeth and freckles. Shelby Aisel has shiny black hair and thick eyebrows. Frederica Alberts has glasses and short, spiky hair.

By 8:26 a.m. I've gotten to Melody Marsinco. She doesn't have curly hair and a twisted tooth, and neither do any of the other 1,507 female students I've searched.

What if I never find her? I can't remember the last time I felt relaxed talking about music with someone. She made me remember why I fell in love with it, actually. She's unassuming and surprising and unapologetic and real and perfectly imperfect — and that's what makes her so extraordinary.

I think about stopping by Washington Square Park again on Saturday morning, but I have a private lesson with Yaz at ten and there's no way I can get there and back in time. Well, maybe if I take cabs both ways and only stay for a couple of minutes. Or maybe if the A is running express and I run as fast as I can to the park.

Milo's standing in my bedroom doorway, staring. I have no idea how long he's been there. I look up at him — I don't care that I'm still wearing my clothes from the night before, but I can tell he does. "What's up?"

"Mom wants to know if you're eating breakfast with us. I told her probably not, but she wants me to ask you, anyway."

"Yeah, I'll come."

We're having eggs that run out everywhere when you break them up with toast — Milo and I used to call them "goo eggs" when we were kids. And grapefruit juice and cantaloupe slices. Mom puts two eggs on my plate on purpose, even though I never have an appetite in the morning.

Dad's there in his robe, shoveling soggy toast bits up with his fork, and I realize I haven't seen him in a few days. He mostly leaves me alone when I'm in my room, so if I'm working, he'll come home, watch

TV and go to bed without saying goodnight. I think he knows why spending time alone is so important for me. I think it's important for him, too. We have an understanding about stuff like that.

My head is fighting itself all through breakfast. There's the opening of *Kreutzer* thrashing around. And there's A Train and her wild hair, sweetly entering at the end of each phrase. I only have room for a few bites of egg. I get up while everyone's still eating — I can't be late — but my mom groans and presses her fist against the table, and before I realize what's happening, we're fighting again.

"That's it, Ben," Mom snaps. "I'm not playing this game anymore."

My dad is a man of few words, so I know he's upset when he decides to use them.

"Mom is right," Dad says. "You have to start taking better care of yourself. If you keep up this pace, you're going to burn out, and then what?"

"Like last December," Milo says.

My parents freeze, forks in midair.

"Milo," my mom says quietly.

"Sorry," he says.

I know I'm making them all miserable and worried. But I can't help it. I don't know what else to do. If I'm not the best violinist at Brighton, I'll be nobody. But I don't know how to explain that to them, so I force down the rest of my eggs, shrug and go back to my room to get ready.

{ 7 }

Dominique

Third-period chemistry has gone through a phase change. Like, you know when stuff goes from a liquid to a gas? Well, since my life turned upside down, my moderate interest in science has completely evaporated. Who the hell needs to know about moles and uranium and the periodic table? Unless you want to be a scientist or something, how could any of that stuff possibly be useful? Suddenly none of this seems important.

So instead of paying attention to what will be covered on the test next Tuesday, I pick at my split ends and think about Violin Boy. Of course he has a girlfriend. Why wouldn't he? How could a brilliant, hilarious, smart, hot guy like that not have a girlfriend? They probably go to concerts and movie screenings and nice restaurants together all the time. I bet the girl with the red hair is some sort of musical genius, just like him, so they get to keep New York City all to themselves.

"Dominique, will you go up to the board and answer question seven, please?"

I can feel Mr. Valdez and the rest of the class staring at me. I'm still looking down, picking at my hair. There's not even anything on my desk.

"I left my book at home."

"And you forgot to do the homework?"

"My homework was in my book."

"Well, that's convenient."

Anton yells from the back of the class, "She left it in my bedroom!"

The whole class erupts into "oohs" and shrieking laughter. My ears burn. I pull my hair over them, protecting myself from the noise and the shame.

"Anton. Principal — now."

Mr. Valdez is way better at controlling his class than Jenkins is. Anton packs up and everyone's quiet after a few seconds. Valdez forgets about making me go to the board, so I guess Anton did me a favor in some twisted way.

I resume my split-end picking until the bell rings.

＊ ＊

Cass is sitting at our usual lunch table with a tray of cheese fries.

"Found him," he says.

"Who?"

"Who do you think? Ben Tristan, violin virtuoso." With a flourish he pulls a printed page from his pocket and reads out loud: "Started playing when he was four, became the youngest member of the City Youth Chamber Orchestra when he was eight, won the mayor's award for Most Promising Young Talent when he was twelve, traveled to Rome with the youth orchestra when he was fourteen. He's seventeen — graduated from the Dalton School two years early. He's a sophomore this year at Brighton."

"Sounds like a talented dude," I say, trying not to cringe. God, he's so lucky. If I had even one-billionth of the opportunities he had, I'd be dancing at Alvin Ailey right now. "I'm over him, Cass. Really. I don't want to talk about him anymore."

"I just did the best Sherlock Holmes–style sleuthing of my life and you don't even care?"

"Nope."

"I don't get how you can be so totally nonchalant. He's seventeen! Our age!"

"Cass …"

"I know his first and last name. We could probably figure out his address if we really wanted. I could call up Brighton and get his class schedule."

"Cass!"

"What?"

"He has a girlfriend. I saw her."

"Oh. Well, fuck."

"Yeah."

* *

Mom's not expecting me at Spin Cycle until three thirty, so Cass and I take the long way down Broad Street when school lets out. We walk in silence for a few minutes, passing the clumps of kids smoking joints and e-cigs out front. Our school doesn't have the money to offer after-school programs, but even if it did, I doubt anyone would join them. Instead you've got a weird mix of kids who rush out to after-school jobs to help their families, and kids who spend school nights selling weed and Oxy and stirring up trouble.

We stop for a second in the alley next to Adelia's Drugstore. I rest my back against the cool brick and Cass copies me. He offers me his last stick of gum, and I don't know why, but that makes me want to bawl. For someone who never cries, I sure have wanted to do it a lot recently. Cass puts his arm around me. We stand there for a while with the breeze blowing past us.

The apartment in front of us has wooden boards covering the windows and doors. I can't remember the last time someone actually lived there. It's not so bad — give it a few coats of paint and take the old folding chairs off the front lawn and, well, obviously install some windows, and it would be a fine place for a family to live. Then a rat runs out and down the front steps. We both crack up. It's all too perfectly terrible.

Cass squeezes my shoulders. "When we're living at Carnegie Hall or wherever, we're going to think about this exact moment and shove spoonfuls of caviar in our mouths and wash it down with champagne and just laugh so hard. I'll have seven Oscars and you'll be a world-renowned dancer —"

"I quit, remember?"

"You're just on hiatus. Until you can afford to take classes again."

"I don't want to talk about it."

"And we're going to have our own butler. And an indoor tennis court. And did I mention the bowling alley?"

I know he's just trying to make me feel better, but it makes me feel even worse. It's impossible. Even more impossible than the imaginary love story I made up. We're going nowhere. He knows it, I know it. Why bother pretending? In ten years we'll be just where our parents are: buried in an avalanche of debt, working dead-end jobs and barely able to afford groceries. We're stuck and there's nothing we can do about it, no matter how hard we try.

But I can't destroy Cass's dreams. So instead I let him go on and on about our imaginary apartment, all the way to the laundromat.

* *

Mom is exhausted when I get to Spin Cycle, and it's tough to shake the idea that when I look at her, I'm staring at a giant mirror: myself in twenty years. Her hair is tied back in a messy ponytail and her hands are red and dry. She lets out a huge sigh when she sees me, and gives me a pile of sweaters.

"I'm sorry, baby, but I want you here tomorrow night, too," she says. "Dryer six broke this morning and Ralph can't come check it out until next week. I need you on hand-washing duty while I fold and change out the loads. Otherwise I'll be here all night."

"Okay," I say, knowing I owe her about a thousand favors for being so MIA this past week. It's important that I'm here. Not chasing after stupid Violin Boy. Ben.

This is where I belong.

I plunge the sweaters into a basin of icy water, numbing my fingers. If I hold them under long enough, maybe the cold will crawl up my shoulders and numb my brain.

* *

Around seven that night, Mom runs home for a few minutes and returns with some cold rice and beans in a plastic container and a handful of hot sauce packets. We eat on the blue plastic folding table, with newspaper place mats and plastic forks. At first I thought it was fun to eat at Spin Cycle with Mom — like a secret picnic only we were invited to. Now it just seems depressing.

"Do you know anything about websites?" she asks out of nowhere.

"Why?" I ask, with more attitude than I mean to.

"I don't know. Just wondering if there's any way we can get some more business in here."

"We can barely handle the customers we have, especially if the machines are going to break all the time. And websites cost money.

You have to buy a domain and get a designer, and —"

"I don't know, Dom. I was just thinking out loud. Maybe we could try something more high-tech and get some younger customers in here."

"A store without functional dryers doesn't need a website."

"Okay," she says.

And I immediately feel terrible for shooting her down. "Sorry. I shouldn't be so negative. I'm just frustrated."

"I know you are, baby. I want you to be out with your friends right now. Seeing a movie, eating a giant bucket of popcorn slathered with butter —"

"Mom, you know I'm a Twizzlers girl."

"You can have Twizzlers *and* popcorn. And a cherry Coke if you want."

"Okay, that just sounds greedy."

I laugh and hang up a damp sweater. Mom laughs, too, and everything's okay for a minute.

* *

Folding the last few loads takes longer than we thought. We lock up around eleven and walk the three blocks home. Mom carries her Taser (even though I'm pretty sure they're illegal in New Jersey) and I hold my pepper spray. Someone could be ducking behind a parked car, waiting.

"When we first moved here, I swear I thought the Burg would be an up-and-coming neighborhood," Mom says out of the blue.

It's too dark to see most of her face, but her voice sounds sad. Like three-seconds-from-giving-up depressed.

In the distance I can see the Lower Trenton Bridge, with its neon lettering making the water glow red. I can barely make out the words from here, but I know what they say. I've seen the sign almost every day since I was a baby: "Trenton Makes — The World Takes." There used to be all sorts of manufacturers here. There were steel mills and a pottery company and an ironworks. The place was booming. The Burg — Chambersburg, our neighborhood in South Trenton — was full of nice families. Then I don't know what happened. People started moving out to Pennsylvania. Gangs started moving in. And suddenly we looked around and everything was different. Now the sign is more ironic than anything.

"I should have been smarter," she says. "I should never have let your dad decide. I should have gone to the city and taken some business courses and opened my boutique. I could have had my own life instead of getting consumed with his."

She's thinking about what her life would have been like if she'd never had me. But she'd never say those things out loud.

"You did your best," I say. Like I always say when she brings this stuff up.

"We're gonna get you out of here," she whispers.

"I'm fine."

"This isn't fair to you. My mistakes don't have to hold you back. We can look for college scholarships online and apply to every single one of them, and you can go to a top school on a full ride, and ..."

I nod and we keep walking, but I'm not listening anymore. I don't tell her I won't be applying to schools. Only kids with 4.0 GPAs get scholarships. And paying tuition, even for a community college, would put me in too much debt. Besides, the only thing I've ever wanted to do is be a dancer, and that's obviously never going to happen now.

Maybe I could get a corporate job — office manager or something — after I graduate high school, and help Mom out at night. We could save up enough money for her to open her own boutique in Princeton or Hopewell, like she used to dream about when I was a kid. And once it starts getting business, we could hire some other employees. Then she'll only work when she wants to, not because she has to. On her nights off we could hang out at home, making dinner and watching movies and just relaxing. And when she's too old to work anymore, I'll manage the boutique myself and she can retire to South Carolina and get a nice little place by the beach.

Mom deserves to have a good life, and I'll do anything I can to help her. Even if it means working at Spin Cycle every night. So that's it. I've made up my mind. No college. And no dance. And no Ben.

{8}

Ben

Hour who-knows-what of hashing out *Kreutzer* at Claire's house, and I'm so trapped in my head I don't even know what I'm playing anymore. It was light when we got here and now it's dark, and it's way too quiet. There's nothing but static coursing through my brain.

Claire's getting tired and her parents have gone to bed already, probably with earplugs so they don't have to hear the same fourteen bars over and over again. Claire's finally starting to get it, and some of the piece sounds beautiful and painful and sad and shining. Then again, some of it sounds like absolute shit.

"Wait." I rest my chin on my violin and wave my bow at her. "Something was off there, wasn't it?"

"I'm not sure," Claire says. "Want to try from the top of the second variation?"

"I can't pinpoint what it is. Play your part again."

She plays. Then she plays it again.

"What is it?"

"You keep slowing down at bar ninety-seven. Aren't you hearing it?"

"But it's written in the piece. It's right there on the page. How could it be too slow?"

"Beethoven didn't mean *that* slow."

Claire laughs, a high, fluttering laugh that comes off totally condescending, even though I'm not sure she means it to. "Oh, you asked him what he wants? This part is supposed to be slow. Listen to any recording of the piano part there. It's in tempo. I don't know what to tell you."

"I'm not telling you to change the piece, I'm telling you that when I'm trying to get through these sixteenth notes and then you come in with this plodding, stretched-out phrase —"

"Plodding? Okay. You know what, Ben? We need to call it a night."

"But we're only halfway through. We haven't even touched the third movement yet. Robertson's going to skewer us."

"We've been playing for five hours. I need sleep — it's almost eleven. I'm not invincible like you."

"That crap we just played is good enough for you?"

"It's good enough for tonight. Robertson doesn't expect us to be perfect. It's just a check-in. I'm tired and we're obviously not going to get any more productive work done tonight."

"Obviously not." I pack up my violin, not bothering to clean it. Not even the chin rest.

* *

I open the door and carefully put my violin case on the floor by the coat rack. It's late, but Mom's still up reading the *New Yorker* on the couch. Her face falls when she sees me.

"Sweetie, you look exhausted." She jumps up and tries to give me a hug.

"Yeah," I say, shooing her away, because my skin burns and I have a headache and I'm not sure there's anything I can tell her at this point to make her stop worrying. "I'm just gonna go to bed, okay?"

"Did you eat dinner?"

"Yeah," I lie. The living room is too bright and I want to be alone, and honestly, I couldn't tell you if I ate dinner or not. I remember, vaguely, being offered a plate of pasta and salad by Claire's mom, but I did I eat any of it? Maybe a few bites, just to be polite.

The light makes my brain buzz. I have to get out of here.

"I'm going to bed," I repeat. "I'm not feeling great."

"Like, you think you're getting a cold?"

"Yeah," I say quickly, regretting it at once. "Must be coming down with a cold or something. Better get some rest. Claire and I are playing the sonata for Dean Robertson tomorrow. A check-in to make sure we're on track before the audition. It's a pretty big deal."

"Just a cold? That's all?"

"Yeah."

"Do you think you're ready?"

"I'm always ready."

"I'm so proud of you, my talented, brilliant, remarkable boy."

Mom's eyes get all glassy, and I go to my room and shut the door before she can come over and hug me again.

The buzzing is no better in here alone with the door shut. My back is drenched in icy sweat, and it's not even hot outside. I strip down to my boxers and air-dry.

Nothing is right. I want to press Rewind, to go back to when everything in my life was clicking. Back to the amazing Carnegie Hall concert and the effortless inspiration and the unlimited energy.

And the girl at the fountain.

Who is she?

She has to be somewhere.

And just like that, electricity surges through me. Like magic, as soon as I think of her. She makes me feel like myself again.

I have to find her.

I turn on my laptop, open an empty document and pick the biggest font that fits on the page. I type, holding my breath, hands in hyper drive, eyes blurred, until my pinkies cramp up and the whole page is full.

I read my writing over and over again. This is complete and total bullshit. What am I even talking about? She's going to think I'm insane. Maybe I *am* insane.

I delete the whole thing and start again. This is all wrong. My words need to be more lyrical, more emotional, more fun, more exciting. More like her. The way I know she has to be.

I need to find her.

She'd never respect a guy who just sits there doing nothing.

She'd want me to do something grand and sweeping and romantic, like in one of her old movie musicals.

So I print out two hundred copies.

HAVE YOU SEEN THIS GIRL?

1. Wild, curly hair that's so thick you could lose yourself in it. Like, you could take a walk in it for days, months, years and never find your way out. (But smooth and soft, not matted or tangled.)

2. A voice like liquid gold. Like if Norah Jones and Ella Fitzgerald were cloned and their genes were all mixed up together. Not sure if she can actually sing, but if her speaking voice is this good, the sky's the limit.

3. Green backpack. Self-explanatory.

4. A smile that people write songs about. Whole albums. Sonatas. Symphonies. If her smile were a scale, it would undoubtedly be major pentatonic.

5. Answers to "A Train." This is not her name. But if you call her this, she'll probably turn around and smile.

Please send all leads to ...

lookingforatrain@gmail.com

While the flyers are printing, I open a map of the city on my computer and drop virtual pins on every street corner I think A Train could pass during the day. I think about putting a flyer in every subway car — citywide! — but realize I'll need a lot more than two hundred copies and I'm almost out of computer paper. Should I run out to Staples and buy some more? I could buy reams and reams and spend the whole night printing and the whole day papering, and by dinnertime tomorrow, the entire city will be plastered with my signs.

No. I'll start with just two hundred. Let's be realistic here.

She has to see it. Manhattan isn't that big. She's somewhere. I know she's somewhere.

I open my window and crane my head out. Cars shoot by like rockets, headlights blurred and fuzzy, faster than my eyes can process them. Pushing up against the window frame, I extend my whole upper body out the window. The cold air feels so good, tickling my skin, like an air shower.

I could stay like this forever, bathed in the cold, quiet night.

A woman with a stroller and a man with gray hair pass underneath me, walking very, very slow. I try to fast-forward them with my mind, but they won't budge. There's no one with brown, curly hair. No one at all.

Whoa — my right foot slips and my whole body tingles as I grip the sides of the windowsill with my fingertips. Legs scrambling, slipping, I jam my toes into the carpet and brace myself.

I find my balance and ease myself back through the window, into my room. There's a big red line on my stomach, like I've had my appendix out or something. At first it startles me, but then I realize it's just from pressing against the windowsill. I shake my head and try not to think about falling, but my mind is still flashing pictures of me plummeting to my death on Lexington Avenue.

My palms are soaked and my back is all hot, and I think I need to sit down. I just need to sit down.

Sometimes I get like this, that's all. It's not getting worse. It's always like this, and then it gets better and then I'm fine and back to normal. I just need to get through it. I always come out of it. Always.

* *

I tear into the classroom five minutes late, and Claire is already there, sitting at the piano and giving me death stares.

"I can be ready in thirty seconds," I yell, scrambling to sit in the front row and open my violin case at the same time.

"Relax, he went to grab a coffee at the deli. He'll be at least a few more minutes."

"Are you ready?"

"Maybe not according to your standards, but at least I got here on time."

"You're pissed, aren't you?"

"I'm not pissed, thank you very much. I just don't get why I needed a lecture from you last night about the seriousness of this, like I'm not pulling my weight or something — and now you're the one who doesn't freaking show up."

"Let's just call a temporary truce, and we'll talk about it after, okay?"

"I'm shocked that the great Ben Tristan would even want to be in the same room with me after I succumbed to such human vulnerability last night. Excuse me for needing to sleep in order to function."

I don't have an answer for that, so I tune my violin and we sit in silence until Robertson comes in.

Coffee in hand, he takes a seat in the front row of chairs that circle the piano. I stand up, like for some reason, that will make my apology more sincere.

"Mr. Robertson, thank you so much for taking the time this morning. I apologize for the delay. The trains were hell this morning."

"Were you on the N?"

"The 6."

"Oh, God, I don't envy you. Seems like that thing is packed every hour of the day — like sardines in a rolling tin can."

Claire and I both laugh a little too hard. Mr. Robertson ignores us, removes the lid of his cup and blows on the coffee.

"Do you want to play what you have so far?"

Claire takes a deep breath and we both nod.

I raise my bow and begin, soaring through the land mine, followed by Claire's opening chord. We stumble through the first movement — it's even worse than it sounded last night, and I can't pinpoint why. Claire is dragging again, but I manage to speed her up. She's following my lead — but why does the playing sound so scattered? I focus so hard it hurts, clenching my teeth to stay in sync with her as we criss-cross phrases, running into each other's lines and overflowing into the room, all jumbled and beautiful — but wrong.

This is so strange. No matter how hard I listen I can't figure out what's wrong with it.

And then it's over.

I pull the violin from under my chin and Claire takes her hands off the keys and we sit, immersed in this great, astounding silence. The nothingness after so much something.

For a minute Robertson doesn't say a word.

Then he looks at his hands.

Finally he speaks.

"Well, this could use some work," he says.

"It was better last night," Claire blurts out.

"Barely," I snap back.

"You need to listen to each other," he continues. "Claire, there were so many moments when you almost had it. The opening was beautiful. Dare I say, astounding. But I can feel you counting. Just get out of your head and run with it. I want lighter, more effortless, airy."

She puts her head in her hands and her face gets all red — she's so relieved I wonder if she's going to start crying.

"And Ben. Where do I begin?"

Shit. Never in history has the question "Where do I begin?" ended with anything good. I bite my tongue so I won't interrupt him. I wipe my face with the inside of my elbow. My forehead is soaked with sweat.

"You really impressed me at Carnegie Hall. I was at Lincoln Plaza the other night, seeing the new Woody Allen movie, and all at once it hit me. I thought, 'Ben may be the best second-year violinist we have right now. He has the potential to be one of the greats.' "

"Thank you," I say. Here it comes.

"Today I wasn't impressed. You were rushing. You came in early at least twice. I didn't feel you were even in the same room as Claire. What a mess, Ben. Go over it with Yaz as much as you can before the audition. He knows this piece better than anyone. Both of you. Work with your private teachers, work together, work separately. There's plenty of time to get this in good shape before you play it for the rest of the judges at the end of the month. Right now we're looking at thirty-three pairs competing for six slots, so the selection process won't be easy."

"Okay," I say. "Thank you. We'll work on it."

"Thank you both."

Robertson rushes out with his coffee cup and backpack to make it to the Rose Building before his next orchestra class. And then he's gone and the room is silent and still again.

Claire's lips are turned down in a pout, but her eyes are white lightning.

"I'm sorry," she says.

I can see her head puffing up with arrogance and confidence. But she hasn't earned any of it. She was all over the place in the first movement, and she would have been even more lost without me to guide her. How does Robertson expect me to sound when I'm trying to help her stumble through?

"Sorry for what?" I ask, flashing my smoothest grin.

"I'm sorry Robertson was so hard on you."

"It's fine," I say, because there's nothing else to say.

"He's just trying to challenge you," she says. "He knows your potential and he doesn't want you to get away with doing anything less. So the tempo was weird. We'll get it right. We just need to —"

"Or maybe I just suck," I say, setting my violin in the case and shutting it as fast as I can. I don't wait to hear her response. I'm already walking down the hallway and through the big glass doors.

Robertson must have made a mistake. He must have heard me trying to speed Claire up, which made him think I was rushing or I didn't know the phrase. He didn't understand what I was trying to do.

I stalk past the fountain. The first two bars were perfect. Perfect. One of the most difficult introductions of any violin piece in the history of classical music, and all he could hear were the tempo issues. Unbelievable.

I'll just have to do better. Play with more passion, more energy, more emotion. I can't let anyone hold me back anymore. Not Claire, not Carter, not Robertson. Nobody.

* *

I start on Fiftieth Street, armed with a roll of packing tape and flyers.

Wait, am I really doing this? Is she going to think this is clever — or just crazy? No. I know she'll love it.

I snake back and forth across the street until I've hit every streetlight and No Parking sign. Then I start down Fifty-First. Then Fifty-Second. Then Fifty-Third. It's starting to get dark, but I don't care. I don't think you're really supposed to stick flyers up in the city, anyway, so maybe it's better that no one can get a good look at my face.

My superhero X-ray vision zooms in across the street on a girl with a puff of dark, curly hair. The light is about to change, so I bolt in front of a white van and race up next to her. It's not A Train. It's a crying, drunk woman yell-slurring at some guy who must be her boyfriend but probably won't be for long.

I keep going, taping a flyer to every sign I pass. Fifty-Fourth. Fifty-Fifth. Fifty-Sixth. Fifty-Seventh. The streetlight on the corner by Carnegie Hall.

An old man with a nose three sizes too big for his face stops me and asks what I'm doing. I hand him a flyer and tell him to keep an eye out for A Train. He scrunches up his gigantic nose and keeps walking. I immediately regret wasting a flyer on him.

My phone buzzes in my pocket. Milo.

I answer it.

"Where the hell are you?"

"Uh, out, why?"

"Mom's really upset."

He's right — I can hear her muffled crying through the phone. "I told her I was going out."

"It's after midnight."

"Wait, it's that late? Damn it, I don't know what happened. Tell her I'm so sorry. I really messed up."

"Just come home, okay?"

"Yeah, be home as fast as I can. Fifteen minutes."

I look at my watch. No way it's after midnight. The last time I looked down it was 7:58 p.m.

I need to stop doing this.

I need to buy a buy a bigger watch.

{ 9 }

Dominique

Sunday night, nine o'clock. I'm eating spaghetti out of the pot. Mom's working late at Spin Cycle, trying to catch up — one of the dryers is still broken and we're waiting for a part to be shipped, so everything's running at half speed. I have a chemistry test tomorrow so she made me stop helping and go home. I hate leaving her there, and I hate being home alone at night just as much.

The apartment gets creepy at night. The neighbors yell and people run up and down the stairs. And even though our place is small, it starts to feel way too empty for just me.

Then I hear a knock at the door. It's so loud the window rattles.

My first reaction is to hide. When I was little, Mom would make me duck behind the couch whenever someone knocked on the door, just in case it was a person who wasn't supposed to be there. She dated a few guys after my dad left, until one guy came around in the middle of the night after she broke up with him.

She never had another boyfriend after that — at least, not that I know of. When I was younger, I always thought it was just that she was too focused on work, but now I realize she's probably been trying to keep me safe.

The knocker pounds again, but this time he calls, "Maria, Maria!" And then he starts singing that song from *West Side Story*. No way it's a crazy gun-wielding murderer. It couldn't be anyone but Cass. I look through the peephole, and even though he's wearing a huge black sweatshirt with the hood on, I definitely see Cass's brown eyes.

I open the door. "Don't you know how to text?"

He races in and pushes me to the couch so hard the spaghetti pot hits the linoleum.

"What's wrong with you?" I bend over to get the fork from under the couch, but he grabs me and pulls me back up.

"Dom! Stop! Read this."

He shoves his phone in my face.

I stare at it. I can hardly speak.

"Where did you see this?" I sputter at last.

"It's on Grave's Instagram."

"Who?"

"Grave. The new counter guy at Lombardo's Pizza."

"His name is Grave?"

"Yeah."

"*Grave*?"

"Okay, yes, that's not the point. Dom, it's viral. It got twenty thousand Likes. Is this you?"

"Whoa."

We run into the bedroom, grab my laptop and spend the next hour crafting a response.

To: lookingforatrain@gmail.com
From: hidingbehindcurls@gmail.com

Subject: Hey
September 30, 10:32 p.m.
I saw the flyer on Instagram. How do I know it's really you?

To: hidingbehindcurls@gmail.com
From: lookingforatrain@gmail.com
Subject: Re: Hey
September 30, 11:03 p.m.
I've gotten 1,479 e-mails to this account since I put the flyers up, so the real question is, how do I know it's really you?

To: lookingforatrain@gmail.com
From: hidingbehindcurls@gmail.com
Subject: Re: Hey
September 30, 11:28 p.m.
Hmm. Good point.

To: hidingbehindcurls@gmail.com
From: lookingforatrain@gmail.com
Subject: Re: Hey
September 31, 12:14 a.m.
Here's what I'm telling everyone who e-mails: I'll be standing where we first met at eight o'clock tomorrow night. If it's really you (and it's really me), we'll both be there.

He's been looking for me. He thinks my voice sounds like liquid gold. I say the words, just to see if he's right.

"He's been looking for me."

Like a burst of light in the dark sky. A firework, exploding in the distance.

* *

Monday is the night everything changes forever.

Cass spots me the cash for yet another train ticket. Damn, I owe him. I feel terrible taking his money, especially because I know he doesn't have any, but he insists, and my heart is so trembly and my hands are so shaky I don't know what else to do. So I let him pay, and then we're on the train to Manhattan together, me fidgeting all over the place and Cass gripping my hand. He's doing double duty as my moral support and my bodyguard.

"Should I tell him I'm eighteen or nineteen?" I ask. "Do you think twenty is pushing it?"

"Why don't you just tell him the truth?"

"So I tell him I'm actually in high school and I live in Trenton with my mom in a crappy third-floor walk-up, and if I really play my cards right, someday I'll inherit a laundromat?"

Cass pauses. "You're right. Lying is your only option."

"Besides, it's not like I'm going to get married to this guy or something."

"You never know."

"Shut up."

"So you go to NYU."

"Yeah, and I live in Goddard Hall and I'm studying to get my bachelor of fine arts in dance. I have to take regular classes, too, like comparative literature and biology and a bunch of lectures and seminars. My roommate's name is Samantha and she's premed, and our dorm overlooks the park. It can be a little loud, especially at night, but I love living right in the middle of everything."

"So you've given some thought to this."

"I've given this some thought. And three hours of Google research."

Ben Tristan. Ben Tristan the violinist is looking for me.

I notice my reflection in the train window. My hair is frizzing everywhere, and I have a zit on my nose, and my forehead is all shiny, and my eyes are bugging out and bloodshot, and my neck has these weird, horizontal lines on them, and my shirt is too big and there's a little hole near the hem, and my butt is a freaking boulder, and there's no possible way I can meet Ben Tristan right now. No way.

"Let's go back," I say to Cass. "I changed my mind."

"What are you talking about? We're halfway there."

"Forget it — I don't want to go. I can't do this."

Cass grabs my hand and doesn't say anything. I can feel my cold fingers shaking against his still, warm ones.

The train zooms through the suburbs, whether I like it or not.

In an hour I'll be standing next to him.

{ 10 }

Ben

Mom asks me to clean my room on Monday, and instead of just cramming a bunch of junk in my drawers like I usually do, I actually fold the sweaters and take the plastic off my dry-cleaned dress shirts and bring my empty water glass to the kitchen to put in the dishwasher. I finish in record time and spend the next hour practicing. Well, trying to. It's weird, because I never get stage fright, but every time I remember I'm about to meet A Train at eight, my fingers start trembling.

I give up after forty-five minutes of being totally unproductive. I can't remember the last time I was this nervous. Maybe my first kiss with Juliette, a girl from orchestra camp I kind of dated for a few months. Our braces kept clicking together, so it was hard to feel any of that stuff you're supposed to feel. I haven't really had a girlfriend since her. That was three years ago now. I'm definitely overdue.

This is useless. I can't do anything but pace around the room and worry, so I put my legs to better use — I walk the seven avenue blocks and thirty-two street blocks from our apartment to Lincoln Center.

The sun falls behind the skyline, making the sky bleed orange. Like the skyscrapers are on fire, sizzling and hazy. A boy on a skateboard glides past me, followed by a little old lady with purple hair and an even purpler fur coat.

I can't wait to walk up and see A Train smiling by the fountain, waiting for me. Calm rushes over me, and I remember how I felt when it was just the two of us, leaning against the concrete, talking about music. Not about metronomes and measures, but what's actually in our souls. Trading a little part of hers for a little part of mine.

By the time I get to Eighty-Third and Amsterdam the sun has faded completely, and the cabs flip on their headlights. Nighttime in New York City is completely different from nighttime in the rest of the world because there are barely any stars. We still live in the same apartment we did when I was a baby, so it's not like I'm an expert on what other skies look like. But when characters in movies stare up at the sky at night (or when I did that time my family took a vacation to Vermont for a week), they see a whole spattering of stars all over the place. In New York, I can see the thousands of twinkling lights from apartments with everyone home and safe and finishing up dinner. And office buildings that for some reason keep their lights on 24/7 with no one but security guards inside. It's not exactly the same as stars, but I like it even better.

I belong here. I'm part of the city's constellation. I'm the shining buckle of Orion's belt. Or at least one of his toes. I'm not picky.

* *

I'm at the fountain by 7:36. She's not here yet. *Kreutzer* plays in my earbuds. I keep skipping back to the first few seconds of the first movement so I can imprint the notes in my brain. Deep inside my nerves, so I don't even have to think or feel — so they just appear, like sparks, out of my fingertips. But so far it's still not happening.

My phone buzzes and I jump. At first I think it must be her, even though I still don't have her number.

It's a text from Yaz.

Kreutzer is a tough one. Do you want to come by for an extra lesson this week?

Robertson must have told him about the check-in with Claire. He must have told him that it was my fault. Yaz thinks I need extra help now. Fantastic. I try to push the thought out of my mind for now. When A Train gets here, none of this will matter. But the longer I wait the more it keeps creeping back in.

It's 7:52.

Where is she?

Maybe none of the e-mails were really her. Not even that one e-mail I was absolutely, positively sure of.

My skin burns. Maybe the flyers were a stupid idea. Most of them have already been ripped down, probably by cops or street cleaners, but there are still a few up near Lincoln Center. I saw some on Sixty-Third Street, tattered and wind whipped, but you could still read them. I consider running out of Lincoln Center and up and down every street, destroying all the flyers in a burst of torn-up confetti. And then I think: If this isn't her, then maybe I should keep them up, just in case she does see them. Even if it means I get three thousand more e-mails.

It's 7:54.

She isn't coming. I can feel it.

I've checked my watch at least five hundred times in the last fifteen minutes. My mom would be so proud.

Then 7:55. Then 7:56. Then 7:57. Nothing.

I try to think about anything else but her. *Seinfeld* reruns. Those guys on the subway who sing "The Lion Sleeps Tonight" in doo-wop harmony. The first movement of *Kreutzer*, which I still can't seem to master even though I've practiced it thousands of times.

Then 7:58.

Then 7:59.

And there she is, walking up the stone steps with her wild hair and kind eyes and a green backpack slung over one shoulder. She's walking with a tall black guy wearing the biggest sweatshirt I've ever seen. He has a diamond (or what looks like a diamond) stud in one ear and he's exuding so much flat-out cool that it makes me feel like the world's biggest nerd. I look down at the jeans my mom bought me from J. Crew, my stupid button-down. Why did I wear this? I lean my elbows back against the stone ledge of the fountain to try to look more relaxed and less totally freaking awkward.

Here she is with this guy and I'm expecting she's going to want to hang out with me? Right. She's here to say she's flattered but no, thanks, and this is her new boyfriend she met at orientation week, and they're going out to drink mimosas at brunch tomorrow morning, so bye.

Instead the sweatshirt guy stops on the steps, and A Train keeps walking to the fountain, to me. Her. She's the most beautiful thing I've ever seen in my life, all curls and curves, but she's not smiling.

I knew it.

But then she walks up next to me and puts her palm and all its warm, silky softness on top of my hand.

I'm not sure whether she wants to shake my hand or hold it, so I'm stuck doing some sort of weird tense-fingered hand thing on her wrist that neither of us wants me to be doing.

She takes her hand back and this time tries resting her palm on my elbow. She's smiling.

"Hi," she says.

"I'm Ben," I say.

"I know."

"I found you," I tell her.

"So when we met, you felt —"

"I can't stop thinking about you. All week it was like —"

"Like nothing else mattered."

"Like sparklers in the dark."

"Like stars."

"What's your name? I don't want to lose you again."

"Dominique."

Dominique. Dominique. Dominique. It washes over me like rain.

"The flyers," I say. "You didn't think it was —"

"No."

"You sure?"

"They were perfect."

Her eyes are gray, with the tiniest of gold flecks. I didn't notice that before.

"This is my school," I say, pointing to the glass building across campus.

"Brighton."

"Yeah, you know it?"

"Isn't it, like, the best school in the world for musicians?"

I wonder if that matters to her. If that scores me any bonus points. I brush her compliment off, like Brighton's no big deal.

"I guess, yeah. For classical. I play the violin. Been playing since I was little."

"You guess." She nudges me with her elbow. "You guess? You're practically famous."

"No, there are, like, fifty other violinists. It's not as big a deal as it seems." My arm tingles where she nudged me. I wish she'd do it again. "What's your major at NYU?" I ask.

"Oh. Dance."

"So if I say something you don't like, you could high-kick me in the face right now?"

"Most definitely," she says, with a little smile like she just might. This girl is the best.

"Is it a conservatory program?" I ask.

"What?"

"Like, do you only take dance and performance classes, or do you have to take normal courses, like English and all that, too?"

"Normal courses. Like English and organic history and everything."

"So, is that your security detail?" I ask, pointing at the dude on the steps. He's deeply engrossed in his phone, playing a game or doing some serious texting.

"Him?"

She laughs, and all I want for the rest of my life is to hear that sound.

"That's just Cass. He's my best friend. And yeah, he's pretty much here in case you turn out to be a wacko."

"Well, you're in luck, A Train. You can let Cass know I'm only 25 percent whacked, thank you very much."

"Is that the part of you that hangs up flyers all over the city to search for a girl you just met?"

"And the part that wants to ask that beautiful girl out on a date." And the part that wants to kiss her. But I don't say that part.

That sly smile again. "Where would we go?"

I know exactly the place. I've been thinking about it all day. "The Village Vanguard. It's this amazing little jazz club in the West Village, right near NYU. They play all the standards we were talking about, all the old musical ones. And they can play anything. So if there's a song you love and you'd want to hear live, we could request it. I could pick you up at your dorm and we could —"

"No. No, I'll meet you there."

That works. "Really? You'll go?" I take a huge gulp of air and realize

I've been holding my breath this whole time. But I'm not nervous or stressed. More like too excited to remember how my body operates.

"Yeah, I'll totally go," she says. "When?"

"As soon as possible. What about right now?"

"I can't."

"Next Monday?"

She takes a decades-long pause and then says, "I could do Monday."

The four most beautiful words in the English language.

"Let's do Monday," I say, trying not to let on how incredibly freaking excited I am.

Monday. Next Monday. I want to run around the fountain fifty-two times — no, I want to do cartwheels all around it. Honestly, I'm not even sure I can do a cartwheel. But I'll learn how just for this very moment. I don't care if anyone sees me. I don't even care if I trip and fall into the fountain.

And then she looks at her watch.

"Shoot, I have to go," she says.

"Wait. Can I have your number?"

She takes out her phone, I take out mine and we swap. Her phone screen is shattered.

"Whoa, what happened?"

"Dropped it."

"We could go get it fixed. The Apple store's right —"

"I really have to go," she says, taking her phone back.

Dominique waves at her friend and he stands. I can't believe it's over already.

She slings her backpack over her shoulder and smiles. I feel it in my toes.

"See you Monday," she says. Then she walks down the steps.

Her friend shows her something on his phone screen and they both smile.

I watch as they go down the sidewalk and down the subway stairs. My phone is still in my hand, her name glowing blue in the darkness.

Dominique.

Second Movement
Andante con variazioni

{ 11 }

Dominique

"God, that was so mortifying."

"No, it wasn't."

"That was the most mortifying moment of my entire life."

"It was fine."

"Do you remember that time the button popped off my jeans in algebra and hit Mark Rodriguez in the forehead?"

"That was bad."

"If that happened every day for the rest of my life, it still wouldn't be as mortifying as tonight."

"I mean, at some point you'd run out of buttons."

"You could tell he thought I was the biggest dork that ever existed."

"Why, because of the —"

Ugh. I was so nervous and shaky and sweaty I was afraid I'd throw up all over him if I said too much, and he was … perfect, with messy hair and beautiful dark eyes and the clearest skin. The fountain is more unbelievably beautiful at night, if that's even possible. It lights up, and as the streams of water shoot into the air, it creates this sort of glowing liquid sculpture. Grand concert halls surrounded us on all sides. Tall buildings with glass fronts and golden light spilling through every window. To think he's probably played music inside every one of them …

I can't believe we even went in the first place. We were only there for what, twenty minutes, before we had to leave to make the 9:25 train back to Trenton. I should have just stayed home and helped my mom. I bet Ben regrets putting up all those flyers anyway.

"Dom, it wasn't that bad. Trust me."

Cass hands our return tickets to the train conductor as she passes by. She uses a little metal punch to put a hole in each one, then wedges both into a slot at the top of the seat.

"Cass. He asked me what class I have tomorrow morning and I said organic history."

"But —"

"Organic. History. What the hell is that — the history of lettuce?"

"You were just nervous."

"And when he introduced himself, I said, 'I know.' Like I'm some stalker who's been collecting pieces of his dead skin in a mason jar for the last few weeks. I know? I *know*? Either I'm a psychic or a psycho. Those are the only two possible answers."

"So you were a little nervous, but you were great. He has your phone number. That's all that matters."

"He's probably deleting it as we speak."

Cass wraps his arms around me, trapping me in a tight bear hug that I try (but fail) to squirm my way out of.

"It's all going to be fine," he says. "He'll text."

"And that's when he'll find out that I don't actually go to NYU and I've been completely wasting his time. Unless my mom finds out first, in which case I'll never be allowed out of my apartment again, anyway, so I guess it doesn't really matter."

"Dom! You and Ben Tristan are hanging out next week. Forget the rest and enjoy it."

I'm trying so hard to be happy. But instead I just feel like I've made a giant, irreversible mistake. Ben Tristan doesn't have a crush on me. He has a crush on Dominique the NYU student who lives by Washington Square Park and studies dance and apparently minors in the history of vegetables. The first thing Cass and I did when we got to the train station was deactivate my Facebook account, just in case. Thank goodness no other information about me comes up when you Google my name. At least, I don't think so. What if something was posted since the last time we checked?

"Wait, Cass, Google me one more time."

"You're all clear. Just some Dominique Hall in Hawaii who's apparently won a lot of horseback riding competitions. You never had a Twitter account, did you?"

"No. But what if something pops up later, in like a few weeks? Like the school honor roll or something?"

"Relax. I've looked through the first ten pages and nothing's come up that's actually you."

"Best-case scenario, how long could this possibly go on before he finds out? Two weeks, three?"

"Dom, are you kidding me? Relax, every good movie relationship from the last one hundred years has been based on lies. This is so *Roman Holiday*. If you squint, Ben sorta looks like a young, shaggy-haired Gregory Peck, doesn't he?"

Cass kisses me on the cheek, then lays his head on my shoulder as the train rumbles through darkness dotted with streetlights: New Jersey at night.

Ben Tristan. Ben Tristan wants to take me out on a date next week. My whole hand is trembling, my nerve endings alive and dancing after touching his skin even just for a second. I take a deep breath.

"Cass?"

"What's up, buttercup?"

"You're the best."

"I am pretty great, aren't I?"

"Don't get cocky."

* *

It's not until I get home and I see Mom sitting on the couch, hunched over the coffee table with a pile of papers and her ratty budget notebook, that the panic sets in. My skin gets cold and my heart feels like it's going to spontaneously combust. I can't breathe. Act normal. Act normal.

She looks up when I open the door and sighs. She knows something's up. She has to.

"Baby, you're late."

"Sorry, I know. The movie went longer than we thought."

She knows we'd never watch a movie at Cass's house. His mom's always passed out on the couch and he shares his room with his three little brothers. So we told her we were going to Kandice's — my mom has always liked her because she gets straight As. Kandice can make her voice sound a lot like her mom's on the phone and she doesn't mind covering for us, so most of the time when Cass and I are somewhere we're not supposed to be, we say we're at Kandice's.

"What did you watch?"

"*Roman Holiday.*"

"Again? Haven't you guys seen that one already?"

"Yeah."

Mom sighs again, and I know that's the universal sign for "I have way too much to do." It's my week to sleep in the bed, so I haul my backpack into the bedroom and root around for a clean pair of PJ pants.

It's not until I turn out the lights, yell goodnight to my mom and pull up the covers that the magnitude of tonight, the great enormity of what I've done, really hits me. It was real. Everything actually happened. And for the first time all night I let my worries and insecurities fade away. He makes me feel like a different person, the person I want to be. Like I'm the sophisticated star of my own movie musical about New York City. Everything else stops when I'm standing next to him, and it's just the two of us, preserved on film.

When I shut my eyes, he's all I can see. Dark hair falling in his dark eyes, framed by dark eyelashes. A spray of freckles dotting his nose, freckles I hadn't noticed before. His smile: straight teeth, probably from braces, and white with smooth edges. His skin, as white as his teeth, with just a few blue and purple veins peeking through around his eyes. I remember touching his shoulder, I think — or was it his elbow? Just thinking about it tickles my palm and radiates heat through my fingertips.

My eyes snap open.

There's no way he'll find out who I really am, is there? He doesn't even know my last name. There are probably tens of thousands of kids at NYU. A hundred Dominiques, at least. There's no reason he wouldn't trust me.

Well, except for the small fact that I'm lying about everything.

{ I 2 }

Ben

I'm running late, but as I tear through the front lobby, I realize something is different. I think I'm starting to become "avoid eye contact" famous at school. Word must be spreading about the Carnegie Hall concert. As I run by, I see them carefully trying to sneak glances at me. Like a museum exhibit. Too rare to be touched. No one but Claire witnessed the *Kreutzer* rehearsal disaster, so it's not too late. Everyone knows I'm still the best second-year violinist. I can feel it.

And I bask in it, soak, revel — not going to lie. Seas of students part for me as I run down the hallway. Jamie, this girl I've always suspected has a crush on me, shakes her head and blushes when I get on the elevator with her.

And then.

And then it happens.

A white cane stops the elevator from closing. The door shoots back open and there's my hero, dressed in a striped button-down and a sport coat. My idol. Isaac Nadelstein. The man I dare not breathe near.

I spend my nights awake, rewinding and replaying his performances until my ears are numb and the notes have been seared into my brain cells. He's here. His powerful fingers are here; his violin is here in its case. He has everything he needs to play the *Kreutzer* Sonata, just as he played it on that life-changing recording. Everything is right here, with me, inside a six-foot-wide box in the sky.

He can't see me. Well, he can't see anyone, ever — he's blind. They say that's what makes him such a brilliant violinist. No distractions, just the music. They say he can play any piece in the world just by listening to it once. And he plays everything from memory, even Ravel's *Tzigane*. One of the most legendary violinists in history — a classical music god — and here he is, standing three inches from me.

So I don't even think. I just do it.

"Mr. Nadelstein," I blurt out. Jamie looks at the floor.

Nadelstein looks up, opens his mouth, says nothing, closes it again, then clasps his fingers together, all in three seconds.

"You've saved my life in so many ways," I tell him, not sure where I'm going with this. "It's just — at first I was the type of player who just sawed through the notes, I thought the notes were the important part, but now I understand it's the panic, it's the pain, it's the joy. Every emotion I feel gets stored away in some dark corner and gets saved and condensed, uh, and it all goes into my music now. Or I try, at least. Trying is the first step. Thanks to you. So thank you. Thank you, sir." I do this weird bow, like he's the king and I'm a mere servant, and maybe I am, because the only thing I want is to see him smile.

"Thank you, Ben," Nadelstein says.

Holy crap. Nadelstein *knows* me. I probably shouldn't have done it, shouldn't have gushed so much, but I can't stop smiling. He knows my voice. My idol knows me, just like everyone here knows me. I can't wait to tell Dominique.

I beam at Nadelstein's white cane until the doors open and it disappears.

The doors close.

* *

For the first time in my life I'm late to class. It's just theory — it's not like it matters, not like it's a performance class or an audition or something. But when I walk in, Claire gasps and covers her mouth, and I can tell that behind her fingers she's got a big stupid grin on her face. Maybe because she's uncomfortable, or maybe because she hates me now, or maybe because she gets a kick out of seeing me fail, or maybe a little of all three.

And Carter is the worst of all. The only seat left is the one right next to him, so I shuffle past the rest of the row, trying not to knock anyone's books on the floor. He takes his backpack off the empty chair and acts like it's some big favor, sighing and huffing like I'm bothering him. I don't understand what his problem is. I've never done anything to him. Well, except be a better violin player, and I don't know what he expects me to do about that.

So I sit down in my seat — and realize my backpack is empty. Well, there's my violin, and a notebook with some loose sheet music, but none of my theory books. Meeting Dominique (I can't stop saying her name — Dominique, Dominique) got me so excited to work on *Kreutzer* I ran right home last night to practice. Then I got so caught up in the first movement that I went to bed too late. Again. And I must have slept through my alarm, because suddenly it was 9:15 and I was late and running out of the apartment without any of my books. Shit. Carter reads my mind and pushes his theory textbook onto my desk, making a huge deal of pointing with his pencil to where we are on the page. He even circles the phrase we're looking at, like I'm some kind of moron who can't figure it out.

"Thanks," I mutter.

"Anytime," he says.

Like I owe him something now. Like I've sold my soul to this stupid violinist destined for mediocrity.

Wright just keeps playing phrases on the stereo and ignoring the commotion, but I know she's going to mark me down in the attendance software at the end of class, so all my teachers can see. Three lates count as an absence. Three absences and you fail the course.

Ben Tristan: Late. Doesn't care. Not a serious student. Definitely not as serious as Jun-Yi or Claire. Or Carter.

* *

At the first break I run out to the fountain to check my phone. I don't know why I check it there — maybe so I don't have to have another "we're oh so concerned and worried about you" conversation with Claire. I slept in. So what? Nobody died. The earth will continue to spin on its axis.

I press my shoulder blades into the cold stone of the fountain, trying to absorb A Train's — Dominique's — essence, which I know is still trapped inside. I take my phone off airplane mode. Just a text from Mom, wondering if I remembered to bring the lunch she packed me. I type back, *It's great, thank you.* Probably an avocado-and-tempeh sandwich with local greens on sprouted twelve-grain bread, still sitting in a brown paper bag on the top shelf of our fridge. I'll have to find a way to get rid of it when I go home.

Nothing from Dominique. I check my e-mails, too, just in case. There are two new books Amazon thinks I might like: *Principles of Violin Playing* and *Advanced Scale Exercises.* But nothing from her. Maybe she's waiting for me to text. I should text her now. Or would that seem too desperate? I'm the one who asked her out, so shouldn't she make the next move? I put my phone back in my pocket and try not to think about it. She's going to the Vanguard. She said she would go. She doesn't need to text every second to prove that this is real.

* *

After class Claire is waiting for me by the door. Shit.

"Everything okay?" she asks in this cutesy voice. Like I'm a first grader she needs to keep tabs on.

"Just slept through my alarm, no big deal." God, why did I have to be late? My life has become a school-wide preoccupation. She's found a hairline fracture and she's doing everything she can to pry it open, to see if I'll crack and fall apart. People love to see someone more talented than they are fail. That's all she's doing. It's not personal. It's just the game.

The funny thing is, I don't blame her for a second. I'd probably do it, too, if I had the chance.

"When do you want to run the second movement?" she asks. "I can reserve some space if you're around on Monday."

"Can't Monday," I say. "Have kind of, well … it's this girl I'm going out with."

"Oh, really? I didn't know you had a girlfriend."

"She's not. I mean, not yet."

"Who is she?"

"Just a girl. She goes to NYU. It's not important, okay?"

"Where'd you even meet her? You never do anything but eat, sleep and practice."

"I do other things. I have a whole life you don't know about."

She laughs, and I can tell she doesn't believe me.

I change the subject. I tell her I can fit in an hour to practice first thing tomorrow morning, before my ear-training class, if she feels like getting up that early.

"Don't sleep in again," she says, patting me on the shoulder.

This is the first time I've ever slept in, even once, and now she says it like it's my freaking thing.

She seems jealous. I didn't realize Dominique would affect her this much. Not like I want to date Claire or anything. I guess I've just gotten used to her having a crush on me. It's part of the reason I think we're such good duet partners — the tension. It hasn't helped much recently. It's just … I don't know. It's like the story of Claire and me is waiting, unresolved, like a mosquito bite waiting to be scratched.

{13}
Dominique

You can't wear an old T-shirt on a date to a jazz club with a Brighton violinist. You just can't.

So I have to up my game and get really creative if I'm going to make his eyes bug out of his head tonight. Usually I'd just throw on my cleanest pair of jeans and call it a day. But that's never going to work on a date with Ben.

So I call in reinforcements. Cass comes over before school to help me piece together some semblance of an outfit, but I can tell he doesn't think any of the stuff I own is even remotely right.

"What about the purple shirt with the black leggings?" Cass asks me.

"I was wearing that the first time I met him."

"He's a guy — he probably won't remember."

"There has to be something else. What about this black shirt?"

"There's a bleach stain under the boob."

"Damn."

Cass rummages around in my bottom drawer, where I keep all my reject clothes — the stuff I've grown out of, or the stuff that has a hole in the crotch, or the stuff that Mom has tried to patch up a few too many times.

"What about this?"

He holds up a black silk camisole with a plunging neckline, adorned with lace. It's so wrinkled it's hard to tell it's even a shirt, but I know what it is immediately. I got it at Forever 21. For Anton. He was always asking me to dress sexier. To wear more black. To be like the girls he saw on TV. On my birthday he drove me to Quaker Bridge Mall and he told me we were going to pick out my present. I remember being so excited it might be a ring or a necklace, or even just a nice picture frame for my room. Something I could show everyone and say my boyfriend got for me. But instead he convinced me to get the camisole. Something only he could see. I haven't worn it since.

"I didn't even realize I still had that," I say.

"It's gorgeous! I don't think I've ever seen you wear anything low cut before in your life. Have you ever even worn this?"

"It was a dumb impulse buy. Never had the guts to wear it."

Cass holds it in front of me and gasps. "Dom. This would look astoundingly gorgeous on you. Come on, just try it on."

"That's okay."

"Why did you even invite me over if you're not going to let me help you? Trust me. You'd look incredible in this. Won't you at least try it on?"

"No."

"Please, please, please, just try it on, just see —"

"I said no, Cass!"

I never yell at Cass. In fact, I don't think we've ever gotten into a real fight. Unless you count that time my mom gave him the red ice pop I'd specifically been saving in the freezer when we were ten.

He carefully puts the shirt back in my drawer. "Wow," he says. "Okay, forget it."

"Sorry. It's just not something I'd feel comfortable in, that's all."

"Well, tonight is about breaking out of your comfort zone. It's about smashing it on the ground into a billion little pieces and never looking back."

"Okay," I say. "You win. Whatever."

"So you're going to wear that hot lacy thing?"

"No. I have a better idea."

* *

Mom's still asleep, so we have to tiptoe past the bedroom, avoid the creaky floorboard by the coffee table and open the front door in slow motion to keep it from squeaking. Outside, the sun is just starting to peek over the roof of the brick apartment building across the street. It casts a dreamy glow on the cracked blacktop as we walk. In the morning Trenton actually feels peaceful.

"Are we doing what I think we're doing?" Cass asks as we turn the corner.

"Probably."

"You know I'm sneaky, but even I have my limits, Dom. Are you sure you want to do this? If your mom finds out, won't she be pissed?"

"She's never caught me before."

He jabs me in the arm with his elbow. "You've done it before?"

"Only once, before my first date with Anton."

"And we all remember how well that turned out."

"It'll be fine. We'll borrow something from one of the loads that won't be picked up until Friday, so I'll have plenty of time to return it."

"We?"

"Me. This is my decision."

"It's up to you. I thought you would've looked freaking incredible in the camisole, but what the hell do I know? I'm only your best friend and fashion consultant."

I jiggle the key in the lock of the laundromat and pry the door open. I turn the lights on and head to the back room. The bundles of dirty clothes are on a shelf on the left, and the bags of clean items are on the right. I look at the tags on the clean bags until I see the bright orange one I'm looking for.

Cass stands in the doorway, shaking his head. Maybe I shouldn't have told him, but it didn't seem like that big of a deal at the time. I'll wash it afterward. It's not like I'm going to wear it, get it all sweaty and then just put it back in with the clean stuff. Besides, it's not like it belongs to a total stranger or something.

I pull a silky floral shirt out of the bag and Cass gasps.

"Wait, is that … It's not!"

"Yep. Her mom brought in their laundry yesterday."

"Her" is Monica Bryan, a senior at Trenton that Cass and I are completely in awe of. She has this bouncy, shiny black hair that looks like spun silk, and when she passes you in the hallway, she smells faintly of strawberries. In fact, the entire damn hallway smells like strawberries for five minutes after she leaves, like the air is still longing for her.

She doesn't walk — she floats. Her laugh is like golden wind chimes. She looks like she could be at least in college, but not, like, old or anything. Her skin is smooth and beautiful, like it's permanently frozen in that sweet spot between breakouts and wrinkles. When Cass and I spot her in the hall, we follow her to her next class, at least ten paces behind, so we can observe her, like a rare bird in the wild.

Naturally, she has no idea we exist. We've never had the guts to introduce ourselves, and even though she seems nice enough, Cass and I are both sure she'd never want to be friends with us.

So when I came in yesterday and saw that Mary Bryan, Monica's mom, had dropped off a bag of laundry, I immediately dug through it to check out the tags. Turns out Monica's stuff mostly has no tags, or old, weird ones from places like Strawbridge & Clothier, so I can only assume she gets her clothes from thrift stores. Maybe even vintage places in New York or Princeton.

She's the same size as me. Of course I could never wear any of her clothes to school. That would be stupid. But she'd never know if I wore just one of her shirts to the Village Vanguard for a few hours, just this once. And for some reason, even though I don't know her, I feel like she wouldn't mind.

Cass raises his right hand, like he's being sworn in: "I, Cass, hereby approve of this terrible decision."

{ 14 }

Ben

I tear through my closet. The Brandenburg Concertos tie, navy with stripes, and the button-down with the pattern like gray graph paper? The black silk *Jupiter* Symphony bow tie? The itchy wool tie Mom got me when I played Vivaldi's *The Four Seasons* — at the Four Seasons Hotel — for some stuffy donors' brunch the youth orchestra was hired to play on Christmas three years ago? Wrong, wrong, wrong.

I have the perfect thing to wear to a million concerts, but nothing to wear on an actual date.

Mom's been organizing every item of our clothing according to some book she read, which involves being a total freak about having everything in the closet arranged by color and length. There's supposed to be a finger-width of space between every shirt and sweater. And when you get rid of something, you're supposed to take the pair of old tuxedo pants or whatever in your arms and hug it, and thank it for serving you well all these years. Sometimes I wonder if my mom has too much time on her hands.

My entire life I've never had a say in how my room looks. Mom wanted our apartment to look like an actual suburban house, so she had plush, cream wall-to-wall carpeting installed in our bedrooms. On the wall opposite my bed there are framed posters from every major concert I've performed in since I was eight: Stravinsky, Strauss, Mahler, Tchaikovsky and Mozart judge every move I make. I wonder what they'd wear on a date.

What if she's wearing jeans and a T-shirt and I'm wearing a wool bow tie?

I settle on a plain, gray-and-white striped button-down and a blue tie. I comb back my sticking-up black hair so it's neat and glossy and slick, then change my mind and mess it up again. She's not neat. She laughs in the face of neat. She's probably going to wear a giant purple T-shirt to the show, and I'm going to embarrass her, all slicked and polished like some mannequin in the window at Barneys. I hate my clothes. I hate that I have to dress up all the time. I don't even know if I own any T-shirts that weren't from some stupid orchestra camp.

"Whoa, it's actually open," I hear Milo say from the hallway. He peeks his head through the door crack.

"What do you think of this?" I ask him. "Honestly."

"Looks a little casual for a concert."

"Not for a concert. For, uh ..."

"For a date? You?"

"Shut up. She goes to NYU. What do you think?"

"Where are you guys going?"

"The Vanguard."

Milo leads me to the mirror, takes off my tie and instructs me to unbutton the top two buttons of my shirt. I button one back up again. He unbuttons my cuffs and rolls up the sleeves so most of my forearms, and the gold watch my dad gave me after my concert in Vienna, are exposed. He runs into his room to get this weird pomade he bought at Bumble and Bumble and rumples my hair with it.

"Much better," Milo says. "You look more like a regular guy now. Wouldn't want her to get to know the real you until at least the fourth date."

"Shut up."

"Who is she?"

"Just some girl."

"The girl from the flyer?"

"How do you know about that?"

"Saw one in your recycling bin. And then four of them on my walk to school. And five on the way back. Couldn't you have just asked for her number, like a normal person?"

"Shut up."

Milo sits cross-legged on my bed. He's not wearing shoes or anything, but I still hate him doing that, messing up the comforter and getting his feet all over the place. I'm mortified that Milo has had more dating experience than I have. He's never had a problem finding girls to go out with him. Aside from Juliette, the clarinet player from youth orchestra who barely said five words to me the entire five months we dated, I've never actually had a girlfriend. I mean, I've held hands and made out with girls from camp and whatever, but that doesn't really count. I don't like thinking about it, because Milo's my younger brother and everything, but I bet he's already beat me in the sex department, too. He probably did it with his first girlfriend, Maddie, from tennis camp, and with Jennifer, who he only started dating this summer.

"Just be careful, okay?" he says.

"You sound like Mom."

"They're worried again. You'd built up their trust, and now, I don't know. There's this weird energy in the apartment. I just don't want you to get in over your head."

He's wrong. I'm fine now. I just didn't understand the balance last year. Being at a new school, I wasn't used to the routine and I went a little overboard with practicing. But I'm fine now. I'm happy. Everything's going right.

But then I open my mouth to tell that to Milo and the words pour out and I can't stop.

"You know what? Sometimes I feel like you guys are setting me up to fail. I'm fine. I'm eating, and I'm sleeping — probably not as much as Mom would want, but I am — and I'm doing well at school again. Like, really well. Everyone likes me. I have friends. I'm practically famous at school from the incredible concert at Carnegie Hall last week that none of you went to. A girl actually likes me — and she's *amazing*. I'm doing better than I've ever done in my entire life. I have more energy, more power, more passion, more everything. Sometimes I look out the window and it's like I can see each individual star aligning itself right over my head, like everything has a purpose and a plan, and there's nowhere else I should be at this exact moment in time but right here, right now, becoming the best fucking violinist Brighton has ever seen."

Milo puts his hand on my arm. He never does that. He never touches me. It stings, and I try to shake him off, but he holds tight.

"That's exactly why they're worried," he says.

* *

I walk from Ninety-Sixth and Lex to the Vanguard because my hands are moving too fast and I know I'd just distract everyone if I took the subway. Not like other people on the train aren't distracting — the guys doing backflips are the worst culprits, closely followed by the man who pulls a battery-powered amp around in a baby stroller and sings off-tune renditions of *Carmen*. Not to be outdone by the lady with the beat-up violin with a No Doubt bumper sticker on the chin rest, who absolutely screeches through "Don't Speak." She's a special kind of hell all her own.

But sometimes when I'm like this, really energized and wanting to work out some violin stuff in my head, it's distracting for other people. My arms flail, and I hum, and tap my fingers and feet, and I'm sure if you're trying to get through this week's copy of *New York* magazine it's not exactly easy to be sitting next to me.

So I walk, all 4.7 miles to 178 Seventh Avenue South, through Central Park and past the carousel, and past Carnegie Hall and New York City Center, and right next to the towering stack of neon signs in Times Square where the ball drops on New Year's, and then past Madison Square Garden — Billy Joel is playing again — and right by my first tutor's apartment (she had this weird, musty coffee breath that made me nauseous, so my mom pulled me out after a year) and down past the Rubin Museum of Art, where my mom tried to make me take meditation classes last winter on my two-month break from Brighton. They told me I needed to find a healthier way of channeling my stress. I thought I was doing great, sitting on that too-hard cushion in the big, cavernous room and breathing in through my nose and out through my mouth. But then the teacher came over and asked me if everything was okay, and I realized the fingers of my left hand had been playing Stravinsky's Violin Concerto in D on the floor.

On Third Street I pass this little old movie theater I must have seen a million times but never really noticed before. Today, as the sun is sinking behind the skyline, it's impossible to miss. It's all lit up with these big, old round lightbulbs I'm not even sure they make anymore. They're playing a bunch of independent movies. With Dominique's favorite, *Singin' in the Rain*, on at midnight.

Shoot. Would she rather be going to see that instead of the show at the Vanguard? I thought she'd want to hear some of her favorite songs live, but maybe she just likes those songs when they're in the movies.

No. If we saw the midnight showing, then we'd be getting home at like two in the morning, and my mom would kill me. I'll have to take her next time. We'll go see *Singin' in the Rain* on a Saturday, when we don't have to get up in the morning. Maybe by then I'll work up the courage to hold her hand for a minute. And maybe even kiss her.

My mind floods with warmth and electricity and … happiness. And before I can realize what I'm doing, I'm speed-playing the entirety of *Kreutzer* in my mind. I'm whipping through the toughest passages and using my heart to show me the way. This is it. This is the way I need to play it. I need to let the love shine through. When Claire and I practice tomorrow, she's going to be shocked. I'll sound exactly like the Isaac Nadelstein recording. If she shuts her eyes, she won't even be able to tell the difference.

And then there's A Train, the glittering light, right in front of me. Dominique. Walking down the street like no one has ever walked down Seventh Avenue in the history of New York City.

{ 1 5 }

Dominique

He's there.

The real, actual Ben is waiting for me under the little red awning, and my stomach lurches a mile in the opposite direction and I don't even know how I'll be able to say a word to this guy, let alone spend an entire night with him. I look down and do a quick outfit check. My sneakers are still tied, and there's only one hole in my jeans — at the knee. I tug Monica Bryan's floral shirt down over my jeans (but not so far down that my boobs pop out). I'm wearing the fake leather jacket that my mom and I share. It's too tight when I button it but fits well enough if I leave it open. I resist the urge to cross my arms as I walk toward him — perfect, effortless, incredible him.

"A Train," he says in the softest, gentlest voice, and nothing else.

"Hey," I say, surprised at my own nonchalance. I sound calm and confident, like the girl I've always wanted to be.

"Ready to have your mind blown?"

"Let's do this."

At that moment I realize I have absolutely no idea what I'm getting into. I see a handwritten sign in a little glass frame next to the door, with the music lineup for the week. Tonight it's the Vanguard Jazz Orchestra, written in block letters and shaded in with red colored pencil.

MONDAY
VANGUARD JAZZ ORCHESTRA 8:30 p.m.

TUESDAY
JOSH ROBIN 8:30 p.m., 10:30 p.m.

WEDNESDAY
THE ODALISQUE QUARTET 7:00 p.m., 9:00 p.m.

THURSDAY
ERIKA FRANKEL 8:30 p.m.

FRIDAY
JAMIE MCDONALD TRIO 8:30 p.m.

SATURDAY
LE CHAT NOIR 8:30 p.m., 10:30 p.m.

SUNDAY
HERBIE COSTELLO 7:00 p.m.

I take a deep breath and smile. We go in.

Ben gives his name to a man at the door, who stamps our hands "under 21" and leads us downstairs, to a little table near the front. The show is already in progress — I count sixteen guys crammed onto the tiny stage, all wearing suit jackets and ties. Trumpets squeal and saxophones honk and it's all a little too loud to talk over. It doesn't sound anything like the music Ben and his classmates played at Carnegie Hall — in fact, I'm kind of shocked he even likes this stuff. But something about how loud and frantic it is reminds me of the subway. Like how all those people are crammed in next to one another, hundreds of bodies pushing their way out, then hundreds more pushing their way in again. Then the ding of the doors and the trains screech away, over and over on a loop. Ben is tapping his fingers on the table and shaking his leg to the beat.

Ben says something, but it comes out muffled.

"What?" I ask.

"These guys have been playing here every Monday for the last fifty years," he repeats, louder. "I used to come here a lot with my grandpa. He died a few years ago, but this place was always his favorite. I try to come every few months and request songs for him. He loved 'Willow Tree' by Fats Waller, so I request that a lot."

"I'm sorry about your grandpa."

"Thanks. I miss him, but he was old and he had an amazing life. I played 'Willow Tree' at his funeral, on the violin, and that was really the best gift I could have given him."

"Is that something you have to do a lot?"

"What do you mean?"

"Play at funerals?"

"Oh, yeah, I do all the big life events. Holidays, weddings, bar mitzvahs, the whole thing. You name it — I've played it. Want me to play your mom's birthday party?"

"Yeah, do you know any Barry Manilow? She's obsessed."

"Really? No, she's not. You can't be serious." He puts his head in his hands and cracks up.

"She loves him. She plays him constantly at —" I almost say Spin Cycle. "At home."

"For your mom, anything. I'll play 'Mandy' on repeat for three days."

We're still laughing when a waiter comes over and asks us if we want anything to drink. Ben doesn't ask me what I'd like, just says, "Two Cokes, please," and I'm secretly relieved he ordered for me, so I don't have to worry about saying, "No, thanks," and explaining that I can't afford to pay for anything. But wait. Maybe he does expect me to pay for it. What if he wants us to split it? What if the bill comes and he asks if I have any cash? What if he was expecting me to pay for the drinks because he paid for the tickets?

If Cass were here, he'd laugh, put his hands on my shoulders and tell me to stop being such a spaz. I try to relax — to ooze confidence, like Monica.

Ben's focus turns back to the stage. He bops his head to the music, hair flying, eyes closed. It reminds me of the moment I first saw him onstage at Carnegie Hall. I try to concentrate on the music, but it's tough when he's sitting there right in front of me, so tangible and beautiful.

Everything is exactly as I hoped it would be, right at this exact moment. I try not to breathe — maybe I can preserve it, just like this, forever.

"You know, this isn't really allowed," Ben whispers in my ear.

"What do you mean?" I whisper back.

"Classical musicians and jazz musicians aren't supposed to mix. Technically, I'm not supposed to like this stuff. I keep it a secret from most people. Sure, Stravinsky borrowed from jazz, and I guess you could say Leonard Bernstein was an amalgamation of the two, but most classical musicians believe jazz improvisation totally taints the piece. That jazz musicians are hacks, using the same generic riffs over and over again, like they don't have the skill or dedication to learn a real piece as it's written. At least, that's what my teachers would say. And most of my friends. I can't really talk about jazz with anyone."

Cass would be proud of me, because I take a deep breath and decide to say something totally out of my comfort zone: "That's the stupidest thing I've ever heard."

Ben's eyes widen and his grin gets huge, flashing eyeteeth, molars, gums, everything. "Why?"

"Because. I mean, I don't know that much about this — you're the expert — but isn't that the cool thing about art? That you're not supposed to follow the rules? What if someone told, I don't know, Beethoven, that he couldn't do anything that hadn't already been done by Mozart?"

He looks at me with these brilliant bug eyes, like I've just invented pizza and offered him a slice.

"Ooh, A Train, you're such a bad influence," he says.

"Sorry."

"Don't be sorry, I love it. My music theory teacher would hate you."

I wonder what everyone else in his life would think about me. His mom. The red-haired girl.

And then the lights come up and the set is over, and we're sipping our Cokes as people order more drinks, go to the bathroom and step outside to smoke. I realize we're the youngest people in here by at least ten years, and we're definitely the only ones not drinking scotch or martinis or white wine. Ben excuses himself to the bathroom, then I do (even though it's only to reapply my lip gloss and give myself a pep talk in the mirror). When I get back, he's ordered us another round of Cokes.

"Do you drink?" he asks.

"Once in a while. Not really."

"Do you smoke?"

"No. Why, do you?"

"If I wanted to kill myself, I'd find a more interesting way."

"Tie yourself to the subway tracks with violin strings?"

"Couldn't tie myself down alone. I'd need an accomplice."

"Don't look at me."

"It's hard to look anywhere else."

If Anton had said those exact words to me, they would have sounded like a line. Leering and invasive and cheap, like a catcall instead of a compliment. But Ben's eyes are soft and kind and his voice is wavering, and I realize he isn't the pickup-line type. I look down at his hands and they're shaking, just like mine.

I open my mouth to respond. The music begins again in a cacophonous blast, totally dissolving any awkwardness.

His eyes linger on mine for another second, then he grins and turns back to the stage. "This is it," he says.

"What is?"

"It's your song, A Train."

{ 16 }

Ben

Her wavy hair spills out over her shoulders and onto this silky blouse that I could keep looking at forever, but it's rude to stare at girls like that and it's probably creepy, and I don't want to be that weird guy who gets caught staring. But she has seriously incredible boobs and I'm not sure what else to do. I look at the stage. Just keep looking at the stage.

Everyone's always criticizing me for talking too much, but the way Dominique looks at me, it's like I could keep talking forever and she'd just keep listening. And she really hears me. Like I'm enough, right here, exactly as I am. And she doesn't want anything back. She's not trying to get a solo, like Claire; or constantly worrying, like my mom; or trying to convince me to be normal, like Milo. I wonder if she even cares about the violin stuff at all. Maybe she'd still want to go out with me even if I was just a regular college kid. At first I'm nervous, but about halfway through the second set I take a deep breath and relax.

{17}

Dominique

He buys the drinks. After all that worrying, it isn't awkward at all. He just sticks a $20 bill on the table and we leave, like it's nothing. I wonder if he has a job besides going to school. I wonder if he's putting himself through college, or if his parents are paying — and if they *are* paying, are they also covering his room and board. I wonder if he lives in dorms, or if he has his own apartment. I guess I wonder a lot of things.

"Can I walk you back to your place?" he says when we're back outside, under the red awning.

"No," I say quickly, abruptly, way too suspiciously. "I'm taking the train."

"But aren't you just over by Washington Square? It's five blocks from here, just down Waverly."

"Um, I'm actually going to my parents' house tonight, in Princeton. Taking the train from Penn Station. My mom needs some help at her store — she runs an antique shop. Did I mention that before?"

He takes a step backward, and a muscly guy walking down the sidewalk with a big gym bag almost runs into him. "Sorry, man, sorry," Ben says. Then to me, "Oh, I didn't mean to keep you out so late. Are you sure you're okay taking the train all the way to Jersey so late?"

"Oh, yeah, I do it all the time," I say, flipping my hair in a way that seems totally natural in my mind but might look totally ridiculous.

"And where's all your stuff? Don't you need a bag or something if you're spending the night?"

"Nope, I still have a bunch of clothes at my parents' house. There's a ton of space there, so …"

Ben looks at me funny, and for a second I think it's all over. He knows. He knows I'm making this whole thing up.

Then he just says, "Huh. Okay. Well, great. I get to spend a few more minutes with you. I'm up on the East Side, on Ninety-Sixth, so we can take the train a few stops together. Ready to go?"

I mentally run over all the new lies I've told. Princeton. House. Parents. Antique store. I hope I can keep everything straight.

We start to walk, and every sweat gland on my body feels like it's shooting out like a fire hose. I wonder if I should take my jacket off, then decide against it. What if I have sweat marks? What if I'm getting horrible pit stains on Monica Bryan's shirt? And worse, what if Ben notices? I keep it on.

Ben talks too much. Like, I think he says fifty words to every one of mine. Meanwhile I'm thinking a billion words a second, but none of them are coming out of my mouth. I'm not sure if he's nervous or just talkative or what, but it makes me feel more at ease. Maybe he just loved the jazz show, or he really likes hanging out with me — I'm not sure. Maybe he's always like this — effervescent and exciting.

We walk down the subway steps and he swipes me through the turnstile on his MetroCard. There's something so nice about getting on a train without thinking about what it's going to cost me.

He's still talking about music, lips moving so fast they're a blur. 'The best thing about jazz is that there's no right and wrong," he tells me. "The skeleton is there — whatever standard. 'My Favorite Things,' let's say. Coltrane."

"Yeah."

"So when you're playing jazz, you have what's on the page — a tune and some chord progressions — and maybe you glance at the page, but you just … go. And that's the music. The music isn't trapped on some page. It's in the air. It only happens that one time, right in this moment, and then it's over, and you can never have it back again. Like a beautiful mistake. Kind of like dance, actually. What's your favorite song to dance to?"

"I used to watch the song 'America' from *West Side Story* like, every day after school for years. Cass and I used to do the dance routines in my living room. There are so many to choose from, but I'd say hands down, it's that."

"Wait, I thought he was your friend from college. You guys knew each other before?"

"Oh, yeah, we've known each other since we were kids. We grew up together. In Princeton."

"Wow, what a crazy coincidence you both ended up at NYU."

Shit, he's getting suspicious again. "Oh, we planned it," I say as casually as I can. "We had a pact — either we both got in or nothing."

Ben looks sad for a second. I love how everything he's feeling is visible in his eyes, like two dark crystal balls.

"You guys seem really close. I wish I had someone like that."

We head for the train platform.

"What do you mean?" I ask. "You have friends at Brighton." You have girls with perfect hair who hold your hand in Central Park.

"I do. They're just … every friend I've ever had is a music friend. So they're also my competition, you know? Friends with motives."

"Yeah," I say, even though I don't really.

"And they're all so stiff and rigid and uptight about everything. They're nice, but sometimes I wish they wouldn't be so afraid to be different. Like you are. You're just so … effortlessly amazing."

I look down at the big yellow line on the edge of the platform, overwhelmed by the compliment. A train whooshes in on the other side and the doors open.

Ben grabs my arm.

"Whoa, what —"

"Sh, one sec," he says.

He points his finger at the train. The doors close, and as the train pulls away from the platform, it makes a high-pitched humming sound.

"Do you hear that?" he asks.

"Hear what?"

"That interval. It's a minor seventh. Most of the trains in New York made after 2005 play a minor seventh as they pull away."

"What's a minor seventh?"

"Well, in *West Side Story*. You know the song 'Somewhere'? The one Maria sings to Tony after —"

"Totally, of course."

"Those first two notes of the song. That's called a minor seventh." Then he sings, in this amazing gravelly, folky voice. "'There's a place for us …'"

"Shoot, I didn't hear it! Wait, I want another one to come by. When's the next train coming?"

"It only happens when they pull out of the station. And you have to listen really carefully, before they zoom away."

We wait six whole minutes for another train to arrive, and when one does, I shut my eyes and listen as closely as I can.

First, there's the recorded announcement: *Stand clear of the closing doors, please.*

Then I hear the notes: *There's a ...*

"Oh, my God! There it is! That was it!"

"Now it'll haunt you. You'll never be able to ride the subway the same way again."

He grins and grabs my hand. Instead of the red-haired girl, it's me. His skin is smooth and cool, with short nails that trace the tops of my knuckles.

This is my place. Twenty feet underground, on a subway platform in Manhattan, people rushing all around us while we stand perfectly still. I've been searching my whole life, and I've finally found it.

Me and him.

Him and me.

Us.

Here.

We get on the next train headed uptown. I hold on to the cold metal pole by the door and he puts his hand on top of mine.

"Check your e-mail when you get to Penn Station," he says. "I made you a playlist, and I thought maybe when you got home you could make me one, too. There's no classical on it. Jazz and some Broadway standards, but also some other stuff I think you'd really like."

"Thanks," I say, hoping you don't have to have a subscription or something to play it. I try to act cool, but I'm so dizzy I don't even know how I'm even still standing.

I catch a glimpse of my reflection in the dark window. I'm beaming. Totally grinning my face off. But no matter how happy I look on the outside, it could never match the surge of happiness in my heart.

I'm not watching a movie. The charming, lovely, magnetic star is me.

{18}

Ben & Dominique

It happens as the 1 train pulls in.

Just as the doors open.

To anyone else, it would look like nothing.

We quickly brush lips, then move apart.

But to us, it's the one thing in the world that's ever really mattered.

The next morning, we'll open our eyes and think of it.

And the next. And the next.

It's what we'll always compare every other beautiful thing to.

Because this is the moment we finally understand.

We're limitless.

And life doesn't need to be lonely.

It can be kind.

It can be a sweet, sparkling kiss, like a sip of cream soda.

{19}

Dominique

Before I can even register what's happening, I'm at Penn Station, standing outside the train, and the train is pulling away and Ben is still inside it, waving. I hear the first two notes of "Somewhere" and know he's hearing them, too.

The first thing I do when I get home is download the playlist, put my headphones into our old laptop and listen. It's like having a direct line from Ben to my ears, and I never want it to stop playing. Mom's in the bedroom, so I download it onto my phone and listen from the couch in the living room. I wrap myself up with blankets and put it on Repeat. I fall asleep to the glow of the songs on the screen.

For Dominique
"Willow Tree" by Fats Waller
"You'll Never Walk Alone" by Louis Armstrong
"My Favorite Things" by John Coltrane
"Manhattan" by Dinah Washington

"Harlem Nocturne" by Sam Taylor

"Handful of Keys" by Fats Waller

"Autumn in New York" by Billie Holiday

"On Broadway" by George Benson

"My Funny Valentine" by Chet Baker

"Lullaby of Broadway" by Ella Fitzgerald

"Take the 'A' Train" by Duke Ellington

{ 2 0 }

Ben

I don't know if you'd call what I did last night "sleep." It was more like a series of fever dreams followed by a frantic 3:50 a.m. run-through of the third variation, followed by four more replays of the Isaac Nadelstein recording and a few minutes of "Take the 'A' Train" because, well, I can't stop thinking about her.

Now it's 6:30 and I can hear Mom in the kitchen, opening cupboard drawers and making coffee, and I know everyone will expect me at breakfast soon, but I don't want to go. I need to buy tickets to *La Bohème*. I've seen it with my parents and Milo a few times, and it's one of my favorite things ever. But it'll be so much better with her. It's been playing in rep with *La Traviata*, and I know Dom will love it. There isn't any dancing, but that first day when she was asking for directions, she said she'd always wanted to go to a show at Lincoln Center. And I want to be the one sitting there, holding her hand, when she does.

I go to the Metropolitan Opera website and type in my credit card number. Well, I guess it's technically my dad's, since he's the one who pays for it, but it's under my name. He says it's important to build up credit when you're young, so when I graduate and I'm auditioning for symphonies, I can buy a ticket to Vienna or China on short notice, or throw down a first month–last month deposit on an apartment. Having my act together is so important — they don't pass out concert violinist jobs to just anyone. You have to be perfect. Educated, mature, confident, well-read, well-traveled, well-spoken, everything.

I get two eighth-row tickets to the matinee of *La Bohème* on October 13, this Saturday, which I'm not sure Dom can even go to, but I hope I can convince her.

And then, right when I'm about to send her a text to ask, I get an e-mail from her:

To: lookingforatrain@gmail.com
From: hidingbehindcurls@gmail.com
Subject: Good mornin'
October 9, 6:28 a.m.
For Ben
"Good Mornin'" from *Singin' in the Rain*
"America" from *West Side Story*
"The Red Blues" from *Silk Stockings*
"Big Spender" from *Sweet Charity*
"Cabaret" from *Cabaret*
"Dancing in the Dark" from *The Band Wagon*
"Hot Honey Rag" from *Chicago*
"Diamonds Are a Girl's Best Friend" from *Gentlemen Prefer Blondes*
"Anything Goes" from *Anything Goes*
"I Got Rhythm" from *An American in Paris*

At first I think it's just a playlist, like I sent her, but then I realize the song titles all link to videos. I watch the first one — it's from *Singin' in the*

Rain, which I realize I probably should have watched by this point but haven't. There are two guys and a woman tap-dancing all over the place — up a flight of stairs and on top of tables and over a couch. I never realized this before, but tap dancers are basically playing miniature drums with their feet — and they're doing it on top of all the regular dancing and singing. I wonder if Dominique can dance like that. I wonder if she'll ever dance for me.

Mom calls me into the kitchen for oatmeal, and I eat a few bites before going back to my room and playing "Good Mornin'" two more times. Then I feel so inspired I have to try the third variation of *Kreutzer* again. I play it three more times before I have to leave for school. My fingers are flying. Every phrase is more beautifully painful than the last. Robertson has no idea what he's talking about.

{2 1}

Dominique

After school Cass and I stop by Lombardo's Pizza. I want to catch him up on everything that happened last night without anyone hearing us. So we're splitting an order of garlic knots and a cherry Coke, and just as I'm about to show him the playlist, my phone buzzes on the table.

"It's your boyfriend," Cass says. "Open it, open it."

I check the text.

"He bought me tickets to something called 'La Bo-heeme' this weekend. At the Met?"

Cass stands up and pounds his palm on the plastic table.

"It's pronounced 'Boh-em.' It's an opera! It's the one the musical *Rent* was based on."

"I've never seen an opera before."

"Me, either."

"What's it like?"

"Well, in *Moonstruck* — did you ever see the movie *Moonstruck*?"

"I don't remember."

"Okay, so in *Moonstruck* the guy from *National Treasure* is obsessed with opera, and it's, like, his favorite thing in the world, so he takes Cher to see an opera at the Met, and it's *La Bohème*, but, like, there's this thing where he doesn't have a hand, and there's all this drama, and —"

"Wait, what? Back up a sec."

"Dom, focus."

A woman in a floral housedress comes up to our table. *"¿Me daría una servilleta?"*

"No hablo español," I say apologetically.

The woman looks surprised, just like everyone always does when I say I can't speak Spanish. I look like the freaking cover model for *Spanish Speakers of Trenton* magazine. But I took French in school and my mom has no time or interest in teaching me about my Ecuadorian side. She's not on speaking terms with my dad, and it's not like he's exactly banging down our door to teach me about South American history. Sometimes I wonder what it would be like to go to Ecuador and meet my dad's relatives. But then I remember I'd have no way of getting in touch with any of them, anyway, and the thought passes.

"A nap-kin," the woman says, over-pronouncing every syllable like I'm the world's biggest idiot. "Do you have a nap-kin?"

"Oh! No, sorry," I say. My face gets hot. I need to learn Spanish.

The woman moves on to the next table. Cass is tearing at his paper plate, looking at the floor. I can tell something's wrong.

"What's up?" I ask.

He sighs. "So, *Moonstruck*. There's this guy, right? And —"

"What's wrong, Cass?"

"Nothing. I'm happy for you."

I try to grab his hand, but he waves me away. He shakes his head, and I realize his eyes are getting wet.

"What is it?" I ask, suddenly afraid. "Please tell me."

"It's just … This is all the stuff we've always dreamed of. It's actually happening for you. You're getting to go to the city and see operas and get dressed up and eat in nice restaurants and do everything we've always wanted to do, and I'm so, *so* thrilled for you. I just thought we'd be doing it together. It's only been a week, and everything's totally changed. You have a boyfriend and this whole new universe, and here I am, waiting for my life to start. I've never even kissed anyone, Dom — did you know that?"

I didn't know that.

"I don't know if I've ever even met someone I want to kiss. How the hell am I supposed to know who I like in this stupid town? I can't even wear that Humphrey Bogart trench coat we spent years searching for — how the hell am I going to get the courage to be myself here?"

Damn. It's the first time he's ever admitted this to me. I've always figured he was gay and he'd tell me when he was ready. But it never occurred to me that he might not even really know — because he's never felt safe enough to figure it out. Since fourth grade, Cass has saved me. He's protected me. He's given me hope. Now he's the one who needs me. More than I even realized. And I have no idea what to do.

"Don't worry," I tell him. "The best part is you have tons of time to figure it out. As soon as we make it to New York — both of us — you can kiss whoever you want, I promise."

"I just miss you, that's all."

I run over to his side of the table, scoot into the booth and give him the biggest hug I've ever given anyone in my life. We sit there together for a minute, arms around each other, watching the old Italian men in the corner who are engrossed in the soccer game on TV. The lady in the housedress plops down at a booth in the corner. The counter guy slides a new pizza into the oven. Cass takes a bite of one of my garlic knots and then I offer him a sip of soda.

"Okay," Cass says, putting on a big smile. "Let's figure out a plan for this weekend. For your Met moment."

I had no idea Cass felt so trapped here. Even more stuck than me. But then he's helping me figure out outfits and the moment passes, and the topic feels too sensitive to bring up all over again. So I just play along, pretending everything's okay, and after a few minutes everything really feels like it *is* okay, and I'm so grateful I can't breathe. Because I can't lose my best friend. He's so much more important than any of this.

But I can't let him hold me back, either.

{2 2}

Ben

Yaz, my private teacher, has one of those cavernous, dusty Upper West Side apartments with built-in bookshelves all the way up to the ceiling, and I'm not sure they ever get cleaned. I always sneeze about fifty times when I'm in there. It's more like a used bookstore than an apartment. I wonder if he's read all the books. I wonder if he's even read a third of them. Sometimes I think I should take one after every lesson, just slip it into my messenger bag, and see if he ever notices. After a year, fifty-two books would be gone. After two years, 104. Would he actually miss *The Rest Is Noise* or *Revolution in the Head* or *Evening in the Palace of Reason*?

Going to Yaz's has been exactly the same since I was eight years old. The doorman opens the front door for me, and he tips his flat doorman hat and asks me if I've performed in any concerts recently. I usually say no, just so I can get upstairs, but sometimes when I'm in the mood to talk, I'll tell him about my trip to Austria or my solo in the annual youth orchestra concert. I know he's humoring me, because he always says, "Great, man, great. I've got to see you play one of these days," but he never does. Sometimes I wonder if I should just drop off some tickets, but it might be embarrassing if he was only trying to be nice this whole time. He probably doesn't care about classical music at all.

Then I take the elevator up to the seventh floor, open the unlocked door to Yaz's apartment and sit in the living room until he's ready. He's usually in his study, practicing his own stuff. He only has a handful of other students. Yaz doesn't tolerate violinists who aren't serious. But ever since eight-year-old me sat down and started sawing away at "Twinkle, Twinkle, Little Star" (which Mozart arranged, by the way), he knew I wasn't going to let him down.

And I never have.

I sit in the living room, practicing the fingering to the third variation without making a sound.

Yaz calls me to the study, and I sit at my usual spot on the stool next to the piano.

"Ben, how has your week been?" he asks.

He's wearing an argyle sweater and brown corduroys, and his curly gray hair is all over the place. I bet he doesn't even own a comb. He just wakes up and lets it do whatever it wants, like the weather. How's Yaz's hair today? Springy, with 40 percent humidity and a 25 percent chance of frizz.

"Everything's amazing, great," I say. "I'm flying. I'm at the third variation, and I'm at the point where I'm just sailing through it. It actually feels easy. I feel like technically I'm the best I've ever been. I can say with complete confidence I'm practicing as much as humanly possible. I'm —"

"Okay, let's put your money where your mouth is."

He tells me that a lot. I think it's probably because it's nicer than telling me to shut up.

I play the pain of Robertson's feedback and the sparks stirring in my stomach from Dom and my confusion about Claire and my frustration with my mom and Milo's weird judgy-ness, and I take it all and funnel it right through my fingers and into the air. It bounces across the spine of every single one of Yaz's dusty, old books. I've been playing for at least twenty minutes, but it feels like a flash of a few seconds. Then it's over. I rest my violin on my shoulder and my bow on my lap.

"Ben."

This is the part of the lesson where Yaz tells me it's astounding, it's beautiful, it's heartbreaking. This is where he says he's never had a student as talented and promising as I am.

He sighs and starts again. "Ben, there's a lot of work to do here."

"I know. But —"

"You've been practicing this regularly? This is the piece you've been mainly working on?"

"Yeah. Constantly. I barely even think about anything else."

"You know I always tell you the truth. And honestly, Ben, the playing feels laborious. Some sections are over-rehearsed, robotic. I can't feel anything. Some parts are frantic, like you're moving at warp speed. It's inconsistent, like you've taken the piece and chopped it up into little bits."

I try to focus on his notes, but I can't. I rub my temples. It's not supposed to go like this. The words I expected him to say were replaced. Erased.

"But … I can't practice any harder. It's physically impossible. It must be something else. Maybe it's my violin. Maybe it's the strings. Was the E sounding out of tune to you? Is that it?"

"Something is off, Ben, and I'm not exactly sure what it is. Maybe we should get Claire in here and the two of you can hash it out together."

"Wait, no, no, no — I shouldn't need her in the room with me. I should be able to go home, rehearse and have it concert-ready."

"Dude." I hate when he calls me dude. "You're still learning. Not everything has to be in hyperdrive all the time."

"But I don't see how bringing Claire in here is going to help. We're practicing fifteen hours a week together, and I spend the entire time dragging her through. Can you teach me my part or not?"

"Ben, let's slow down a little."

Not a chance. "I don't want to slow down. Did you even see me at Carnegie Hall?" I snap. "Why weren't you there?"

"I was out of town for a family emergency. You know I would have been there if I could."

"No one was there. I was incredible, Yaz. The entire orchestra practically bowed down and kissed my shoes when it was over. They worship me now. Everyone at Brighton knows who I am. Everywhere I go, it's like I'm a celebrity. This is the real me." God, I need this to be true.

My brain fuzzes over for a second, and I can't remember whether everyone at Brighton has been staring at me because of the amazing Carnegie Hall concert or because they were remembering — no. It's not important what they think. What's important is how I play, and I've never sounded better. And Yaz has to know that. He has to.

"Last year was a fluke. I choked, whatever. I wish everyone would stop babying me. I'm ready to apply for competitions again. I could do the Queen Elizabeth, or the Prague International, and finally get some momentum here. If I can carry an entire orchestra on my back, and I'm one of the best violinists at Brighton, I just don't understand why no one trusts my interpretation of *Kreutzer*. You're supposed to be helping me, not holding me back."

He leans against the piano and puts his head in his hands. He's silent for a moment. I know I've said too much.

"Why don't we take a break and try a different piece," he says at last.

"I'd rather not."

"I don't know if I want to keep working on *Kreutzer* today."

"Then I don't want to be here."

Screw him. Screw Robertson. Screw everyone. I pack up my violin, slam the door and race down the steps. I hear Yaz fling open the door and call down after me, but I pretend not to hear. The cool wind on West End Avenue smacks my sweaty forehead.

Crap. That didn't go how I wanted at all. At first I think about going back and apologizing, but I know I can't undo what I've already done. Why can't I hear what everyone else is hearing? How could my perception be so off?

What the hell is wrong with me?

I grab my phone, put in my earbuds and turn up *La Bohème*.

{23}

Dominique

Even though I only got four hours of sleep, I practically jump out of bed on Wednesday morning. I promised my mom I'd catch up on washing linens, and I need to clean Monica's shirt before her mom comes to pick up their laundry.

Ugh. Even just admitting I borrowed the shirt in the first place makes me feel like a terrible person. I keep imagining what I'd do if someone wore one of my shirts without telling me. And the truth is, I'd be totally weirded out. There's no way I can do this again. It was a one-time thing. I need to be thankful I didn't get caught. I'll never tell anyone I did it, and that will be that.

As I load sheets into the washer, my mind keeps drifting back to Ben, like a sweet dream I never want to forget. I wonder what he's doing right now. I wonder if he's a night owl or a morning person. I wonder what he eats for breakfast. Is he a waffles or a toast guy?

Only three more days until I get to see him again. Some people would be more excited about the opera, but I'm most excited about the person who'll be sitting next to me.

What do you even wear to an opera? Cass didn't seem clear on it. And what would Ben wear? Probably a suit. I know I definitely shouldn't do it, but it would be so easy to look through a few of the other laundry bags and check if any other customers have a dress in my size.

Then I remember the dry-cleaning rack.

A company ten minutes away comes with a truck and picks up all our dry cleaning. We don't have the space or the equipment to do it ourselves, so they drive it to a warehouse out in Newark somewhere, then bring it back a week later, all wrapped in plastic and smelling like chemicals.

I start to flip through the clothes on the rack, and oh, my God, there's actually a dress in my size there. It's black velvet with a scoop neck and cap sleeves and a stripe of lace trim on the bottom, and it totally looks like a dress someone would wear to an opera in the city. I'm not a huge dress person, but I have to admit it's sleek and sophisticated, and I'd probably look pretty damn good in it. I check the tag — it belongs to someone named J. Wagner. My mom must have processed it, because it's not a name or a dress I remember.

I check the ledger. It was dropped off yesterday. There isn't a dry-cleaning pickup until Monday.

No. I can't do this. I can't start stealing people's clothes.

Then again, it'll just be sitting here for the weekend. And it's not like I'm going to return it dirty or anything. Damn it. No. This is so wrong. I put the dress back on the rack and try to forget about it.

By the time I've washed and dried the shirt along with a bunch of random sheets it's 8:00 a.m. — time to unlock the door for customers. A woman I don't recognize has been waiting outside, and she huffs and puffs as she pushes in a rolling metal cart filled with her overflowing laundry bag. She immediately starts talking to me in Spanish, so I ask her if she can speak English and she lets out this heavy, irritated sigh like I'm inconveniencing her.

"No fabric softener. You have?"

"Yeah," I say, and grab the plastic bottle behind the counter for her. She takes it without saying thank you.

I'm so engrossed in my internal "to take or not to take the dress" struggle I don't even notice Anton and his family walk in. His mom has already put their clothes in, and she's trying to wrangle mini-terrors Freddy and Maria, who are rocking the vending machine. Anton is leaning against one of the dryers, tapping on his phone. Probably playing some shooting game.

Freddy races to the quarter machine and begs his mom to put a dollar in. He has a red-stained ring of fruit punch around his mouth. He's wearing this old baseball cap Anton always used to wear when we'd hang out — Anton must have gotten sick of it and given it to him. Freddy spots me first.

"Hello," he mumbles. He freezes for a second and looks at the ground, then runs back to the vending machine.

I go behind the front desk and pretend I'm busy with paperwork. Really I'm just pushing papers from one part of the desk to the other, then scribbling on a piece of scrap paper, then moving everything back to the other side of the desk again. My eyes are stinging, I don't even know why. It's not like he's going to say something mean to me when his mom is standing right there.

But then she's walking to the counter. Her short hair is plastered down, swept to one side and pinned back in a tiny bun that looks like a cotton ball.

"Hello, Dominique," she says.

She speaks in the softest, friendliest voice, and I wonder how she even spawned those three monsters in the first place.

"Can you believe it? Anton's actually helping his momma with the laundry. Never thought we'd see the day, right?"

Freddy throws a handful of quarters at the vending machine glass, and they fall all over the floor. The other customers stop what they're doing and turn to see what happened.

Anton shakes his head, his lips curling up into a nauseating half grin. Oh, yeah, he's really helping. He doesn't even look up from his phone.

I try to ignore the whole thing and go back to my pretend paperwork. I draw a picture of a girl with curly hair punching herself in the face.

I don't understand why they can't do their laundry someplace else. Couldn't Anton convince his mom to go to the place off Route 1, like basically everyone else in town?

Freddy whines about being hungry and Anton's mom finally gives in, agreeing to let the kids split an egg-and-cheese on a roll from the bodega across the street.

"Anton, baby, you want one?" she asks.

"I'm good," he says.

I hate that she still calls him "baby," exclusively, like he's five years old. That jerk hasn't been a baby in a long time. But then I think about Ben, and realize Anton's basically an infant. He can't do anything for himself, except sell weed and hang around with his friends. His mom will probably be supporting him for the next twenty years. I refuse to look directly at him, but I bet you anything he still hasn't glanced up from his phone one time.

Anton's mom and the brats go across the street, and it's oddly quiet after that. The washers whirr and a TV news anchor talks about the drought in California. I think about what it would be like to live in California, with all those palm trees and convertibles. I wonder if Ben has ever been there, and if he'd have to slather a whole bottle of sunscreen on his skin to keep it from burning.

One of my dryers buzzes and I speed-walk through the store as fast as I can, avoiding Anton. I unload the sheets, which are so hot you can only touch them for a second before they scald your fingerprints off.

Then I hear his voice behind me, his breath wet and prickly on my back. "You do something different with your hair?"

The sensation feels ugly and familiar, and I reflexively whirl around, like a scared animal. He's about an inch from my face, so I take a step back.

"No," I say. "Same as always."

"There's no one in school more beautiful than you are, you know that? And smart. You're like Miss America. You get an A on the chemistry quiz?"

This is how he does it. This is how he'd always draw me back to him. Not this time.

I laugh him off and go back to folding.

"I haven't seen you around much," he says. "You don't ever hang out in front of school anymore."

"I don't smoke. What's there to do out front of school besides smoke?"

"I don't know. Chill."

"Not my scene."

He raises his eyebrow with the notches shaved in it. "Yeah. Not really your scene."

"Nope."

"Heard you've got a boyfriend."

I stop, midfold, holding a hot pillowcase in my hand.

"Yeah," I say at last, carefully, robotically, knowing even the tiniest hint of emotion in my voice could be used against me. Where could he possibly have heard about Ben? No one knows but Cass. Shit. One of his asshole friends could have overheard us at Lombardo's Pizza.

Cass always talks too loud, and I wasn't paying attention to who was coming in and out. Shit. Shit. Shit.

"What's the guy's name?"

I look around the laundromat helplessly, but there's no one to rescue me.

"Since when do you care what I do?"

He leans against the folding table, getting right in my face, hissing in my ear. "Just don't forget who taught you everything you know. You're not some special snowflake, you know that?"

"Get the hell out of my face," I say, pushing him away and ducking back behind the cash register. My face is heating up and my neck is sweating and I know I must be bright red and splotchy.

"You're a piece of trash just like the rest of us, and don't you let some rich boy tell you otherwise. Just because your mom is white, you think you should live on Fifth Avenue? Enjoy the ride while it lasts, baby girl."

My chest is throbbing, and it takes me a second to register why. Then I realize I've basically been holding my breath since Anton came into the store. A tiny part of me deep down knows he's right. I should just give up. Ben would never be interested in me if he didn't think I went to NYU. If he knew I was still in high school. If he knew I lived here and was this poor. And as soon as he finds out who I really am, he'll realize I'm not good enough for him and that will be that.

But then I do one of the bravest things I've ever done: I take a deep breath and push that tiny part of me even deeper. Farther and farther, until all I can feel is Ben, smiling and cheering me on.

"I'm not your baby girl, and if you don't leave in the next thirty seconds, I'm calling the cops," I say in a strong, sharp voice I barely recognize. It's the same voice my mom used when those creepy drug addicts from Parkside Avenue tried to rob the cash register last year. Mom said we had a gun under the counter and they'd better get out of here if they didn't want to be dead. They ran away, then Mom called the cops, turned out the lights and locked the door. We hid under the folding table for forty-five minutes. The cops never came. Eventually, when we'd stopped shaking and it felt safe enough to go home, we counted to ten, held our breaths, then ran into the cold night as fast as we could.

"Whoa, baby. Calm down. We were just talking," Anton says. He repeats this, glancing at the two customers standing by the dryers, staring. "We were just talking."

I shake my head. I open my mouth to let out all the comebacks, the insults — everything I've been saving up for the past year, everything I've been practicing in the mirror, everything I've wanted to shout in his face, to scream until my throat bleeds, everything.

But I'm all out of words.

That twisting grin. The door slams and the bell rings overhead. It's over.

{ 2 4 }

Ben

Friday is a good morning. When I wake up, my mind is still. Quiet. Serene. Like the duck pond in Central Park in February. I'm not worrying about Claire or Yaz or *Kreutzer* — not even the opening phrase — and Dom and I are seeing *La Bohème* in twenty-eight hours. I even eat some breakfast, and my mom makes this huge, exaggerated deal out of it, praising me and saying she's proud of me. Like by eating half a plate of scrambled eggs I've just cured cancer or something.

I run through some scales before my rehearsal with Claire. We haven't been texting each other as much, mostly because of the stuff with Robertson and the shitty rehearsal. But also because I've been more focused on Dominique these days, and I guess I'm not relying on Claire like I used to. I don't know. Whenever I get the urge to text her, I change my mind and text Dom instead.

The practice room is empty, so I set up my sheet music and lift the wooden cover on the piano keys. Someone left an empty coffee cup and a few crumpled napkins on the floor in the corner, so I pick them up and go out into the hallway to find a trash can. There's a jumbled blast of sound when I step outside — a dozen students are all locked away in their own cubbyholes, each playing a different piece. The practice rooms are supposed to be soundproof, but when you're standing out in the hall, the noise from all the separate instruments hits you all at once, like an accidental symphony.

It's 10:06, then 10:07, then 10:08, and no Claire. I wonder if she's trying to punish me for being late to our meeting with Robertson. I wonder if she thinks of me as "the late guy" now, and she calibrates her timetable according to my new reputation. I'm never late, not if I don't have a good reason. She should know that. But … 10:09, 10:10, 10:11.

That's when things start feeling strange again. There's this clock on the wall — one of those round white clocks that no one would have in a house, but for some reason it's the clock to have in all school classrooms. Would a nice grandfather clock, a throw rug and a couch with a couple of pillows interrupt our learning? Aren't my parents paying some huge amount of money for me to be here? Why do we still have to sit on hard plastic chairs and stare at ugly white clocks that tick way too loud?

I cover my ears and tap my feet, trying to distract myself. Just focus on *Kreutzer*. Infuse the second movement into your body. You can do this.

And then there's Claire, through the tiny window in the top of the door. I hear her laugh. I can tell she's with someone else, a guy, but his face is just out of my view. I stand up to see who it is, but I'm not tall enough.

She opens the door, still laughing. Carter is walking down the hall in the opposite direction.

"Good morning," she says breathlessly, like laughing so hard with Carter just knocked all the air out of her. "Did you work on the second movement?"

"What's so funny?"

"Oh, just the pacing in this stupid piece. We were saying, what if Beethoven didn't even like music? What if he just hated music students, so he wrote all these impossible pieces with a million traps to torture us for centuries?"

"Has Carter played *Kreutzer*?"

She unzips her bag, opens the binder with her sheet music and puts it carefully on the music stand. "Oh, I don't think so. We were just looking at some of the passages."

"Since when do you and Carter hang out?"

"He's a good player. His tone is a little hit-or-miss, but on a technical level he's incredible. I don't understand your problem with him, to be honest."

I suck air through my teeth, but it ends up coming out like a snort. "You haven't had to sit next to him while he butchers Mendelssohn."

"Maybe not everyone takes everything as seriously as you do — did you ever think of that? Maybe he was letting you take the lead because he had more important pieces to work on. Maybe he was prioritizing."

"Prioritizing something else over a Carnegie Hall performance — that sounds normal."

"God, why do you twist everything I say into a sarcastic comeback?"

"I just don't understand why you're defending him all of a sudden."

"You don't give him a chance. You don't give anyone a chance."

"I guess not."

She sets the metronome and we start the piece without saying another word.

{25}
Dominique

I knew this was coming. It couldn't possibly last forever.

It's not like Cass has a lot of money. Honestly, I'm not sure where the cash he's been giving me these last few weeks has been coming from. Every time I'd go see Ben, Cass would slip me a twenty, like it was nothing for him. I know he told me he had some birthday money saved up, but I'm not even sure I believe him anymore. So when he finally tells me he's broke, a pain shoots through my chest, even though it's not my money and I don't deserve it and I was lucky to have him to lend it to me in the first place.

But now I don't know what to do about Saturday.

I don't need a lot. The opera ticket is paid for and I told Ben I wouldn't be able to get there in time to eat lunch first, so I won't have to worry about paying for that. It's just the round-trip train ticket and two subway rides. And maybe Ben will even end up paying for one of them.

Just $20. That's all I need.

I look around the house to see if there's anything I can sell at the thrift store. Besides a sapphire ring my mom gave me for my fourteenth birthday, I don't really own anything valuable. No brand-name clothes, no video games, no electronics, no nothing. Unless someone wants to buy Trunkie, the ratty purple elephant with one eye my mom gave me when I was three, I doubt I have anything worth even close to $20.

I walk by the Dollar Plenty after school and consider asking Rico, Mom's old boss, to let me work a couple of hours this week. But I know he'd tell my mom, and then my mom would ask me what I needed the money for, and I'm a terrible liar.

Even though I've gotten better at it recently.

I wish my dad wasn't such an asshole. He should be paying child support, so at the very least my mom could afford to give me an allowance. Then I wouldn't have to go begging my friends and trying to sell things in order to take a stupid trip to New York City.

So I'm sitting in the store alone on Friday night while Mom goes home to grab our dinner: rice and beans (again) with canned tomatoes and warmed-up green beans from a frozen bag. When I was little, I used to call this masterpiece "rice and beans and beans and beans," and right when Mom thought I was done, I'd add one last "and beans," for good measure.

She's heating up everything in the microwave, which will take at least five more minutes. Then she'll do the five-minute walk back to Spin Cycle. So basically, I have ten minutes to decide if I'm going to go through with it or not.

I hate that I'm turning into someone who lies. When I was a kid, I always used to confess to everything, even if it was just using the last Lego when Cass and I were building robots. But as terrible as I feel, I can't even imagine how much worse I'd be if I stayed here. Should I just fold laundry while Ben goes to *La Bohème* alone — or worse, with that red-haired girl? Should I tell Mom that instead of helping her I've been sneaking off to the city? No. I deserve this. I belong there. I do.

Mom always hides a wad of small bills for the cash register inside a blue zip-up pouch at the bottom of a red laundry bag. It's hidden under some old T-shirts that we use as dusting rags so it looks like just another bag full of laundry. I dig around until I find the pouch, then unzip it and take out $20. I stuff it in my pocket, then grab the dress from the dry-cleaning rack and put it in my backpack.

Then Mom is back with dinner, and we eat rice and beans and beans and beans in silence.

{26}

Ben

Dominique is always right on time. Not that I'd mind if she was late. It's just that I can count on her, and I like that. The minute we're supposed to meet she always appears with her hair blowing gently behind her. Like she's always being professionally lit by a movie crew. Incandescent. Luminescent. All the "escents."

For Date Number Four (I'm counting our first two fountain meetings as dates), Milo doesn't help me get dressed. Operas, concerts and Broadway shows are easy. I'm wearing my typical uniform, the same basic outfit I've worn to recitals and auditions since I was seven: suit pants, a suit jacket, a white-collared shirt and a tie. At first I'm nervous she's going to wear her leather jacket again. She's never been to an opera — does she know she's supposed to dress up? Not that I don't like the leather jacket, but I'm afraid we're going to be totally mismatched and it's going to look weird when I try to put my arm around her. Which I totally, definitely will work up the nerve to do before Mimi dies in act 4.

We meet at our usual fountain spot — I love that I can call it that. And just like I knew she would be, she's there right at 1:45, leaning against the stone ledge. I wonder if I should kiss her again. Probably not. It's weird to just all of a sudden kiss someone you haven't seen in a week, even if you've already kissed them once before. You have to ease into it. She has to remember why she even agreed to kiss me in the first place.

She *is* wearing her leather jacket again. But underneath it is this beautiful, flowing black dress that's kind of tight, but not so tight that it looks wrong to wear to the opera. I'd never expect anyone to wear a leather jacket with a fancy dress like that, but somehow, because it's her, it's stunning. One of a kind.

"Hey," she says, smiling so hard it makes me smile, too.

"Hey," I say. "So remember the playlist? Now I'm now realizing I put the songs in the wrong order. Like, you really should start with Ellington and then transition into Coltrane and then maybe save the Waller for a day when you are feeling down and need to laugh. And then maybe Louis Armstrong. Sorry, I should have told you. You listened to them in the order I sent them, didn't you?"

She squinches up her nose at me. "Well ... yeah."

I'm already talking too much. Stop. Talking. So. Much.

But I don't know what else to do. It's not like we can just stand there in silence, so I lead her past the fountain and over to the Metropolitan Opera House, talking her ear off about Puccini and why he's one of the best opera composers of all time, besides Mozart and Verdi and Wagner, obviously.

And then she does it first.

She grabs my hand.

I can feel her pulse. Her fingers dance against mine, and then she takes in a sharp little breath of air. I look at her and she squeezes my hand harder.

"What's wrong?"

She looks like she might cry.

"Every time we meet here I stare at this building and watch all the people in nice clothes go in and out, and I always wonder what it would be like to sit inside. And now I get to be one of those people."

At first I'm confused — if she wanted to go this badly, why didn't she just ask her parents to take her? Princeton's only an hour away. Something doesn't add up. But then I remember that not everyone's parents are as committed to music and the arts as mine. Her parents were probably too busy to take her to stuff like this. I get chills and realize how thankful I am that she's getting to do it all with me. And through her eyes, I get to see it all for the first time again.

I squeeze her hand tighter.

{27}

Dominique

THE METROPOLITAN OPERA PRESENTS

LA BOHÈME

By Giacomo Puccini (1858–1924)
Libretto by Giuseppe Giacosa & Luigi Illica
Based on Henri Murger's novel *Scènes de la vie de bohème*

Conducted by	Dennis Wilcox
Director	Thomas Harding
Set Designer	Anders C. Schmidt
Costume Designer	Georges Joly
Lighting Designer	Danielle Guernon

CAST

(in order of vocal appearance)

Marcello	Alessio Nucci
Rodolfo	Alfred Pouliotte
Colline	Marcel Freud
Schaunard	Nathan Arenas Romero
Benoît/Alcindoro	Jared L. Ring
Mimi	Camilla Alexeyeva
Parpignol	Ronald N. Larson
Musetta	Victoria Thorton
Customhouse Sergeant	Donald M. Peterson
Customhouse Officer	Jordan Felton

I've never seen so many rich people in one place before. A bunch of them are decked out in suits and dresses that probably cost more than our apartment in Trenton. They're all bathed in this golden glow, like the reflection of the fountain has somehow worked its way into the auditorium and is glinting all over the place. It's like watching celebrities on TV when they're all dressed up at the Oscars. It's so weird — the room is packed, but everyone's so cultured and dignified that it's still quiet, even when everyone is talking at once. And no one is eating. You'd think they'd have popcorn and all kinds of snacks, like in a movie, but no one even has a candy bar.

The inside of the theater looks a little bit like Carnegie Hall, but instead of gold, this has more of a deep-red vibe. And instead of a chandelier that looks like the sun, there are these little starbursts made of twinkling crystals everywhere. A few big sparkling clusters hang from the center of the ceiling, and smaller ones are suspended in midair all around. It's just as beautiful as Carnegie Hall, but different. Like a new flavor of ice cream. I wonder if one day I'll ever be lucky enough to see a show at every theater in New York City.

Ben keeps talking about all the other operas he's seen at the Met with his family — *Tosca* and *Manon Lescaut* and *Otello* and *Falstaff.* All at once I feel shy. He's so smart and cultured and confident and energetic and magnetic and exciting. And I'm …

The usher shows us to our seats and they're perfect. For the first time in my life we're not in some cramped balcony all the way in the back — we're on the main floor, where the stage is. At first I try to play it cool, like I've seen a million shows and operas before, but then I notice my hands are fluttering. I press them together to keep them still, but they're cold, so I sit on them to try to warm them up. It's not like I'm nervous, exactly. I feel at ease in the plush, red velvet chairs, surrounded by soft-speaking people. Then I notice something weird: most of the people are white. A few are Asian, and I think I see a black guy in the front by the exit, but for the most part, I'm in a sea of pink faces. I wonder why white people like opera so much, anyway.

Sorry, Cass, but *La Bohème* has nothing to do with Cher or the guy from *National Treasure.* It's this beautiful story about a group of starving artists in Paris on Christmas. Two of the guys are roommates, and the poet, Rodolfo, falls in love with his neighbor Mimi. And then just when it seems like they're all going to live happily ever after, Mimi starts coughing a lot, and you just get this feeling something bad is going to happen.

And then it snows.

I know it's probably just some guy sprinkling scraps of paper onto the stage from the ceiling, but it's the most beautiful, real thing I've ever seen onstage. One white flake falls onto the singers, then another and another and another, and then the whole world is covered and I can almost feel the cold on my cheeks and eyelashes.

And that's when Ben puts his arm around me.

* *

After the opera, Ben really, really wants me to come to his apartment. But I don't think it's because he wants to get me into his room and shut the door, like Anton would. Like most guys probably would. Then my nerves start to set in. Why does he want me there? To meet his parents? But then we're walking side by side out of the opera house, and none of it matters.

As we turn the corner onto Seventy-First Street, a guy in a big, puffy coat pushes past me and I almost wipe out. Ben grabs my arm and steadies me as I get my balance.

"Are you okay?" he asks.

"How do you do this all the time?"

"Do what?"

"It's like you have to get into a big boxing match with the city just to walk down the street. I mean, I know I've lived here awhile, but I don't know if I'll ever get totally used to it."

"That's so weird. You know what, A Train? I've never really thought about it. I've always lived here, so this is what it's always been like."

"And how do you deal with the sirens?"

"Wouldn't be able to sleep without them. They're like a lullaby. Well, not that I sleep much, anyway. I'm kind of chronically sleep deprived, actually."

The city is so small for a minute, just Ben and me walking uptown, alone together.

We stop at a light on Fifth Avenue.

"What do you want to do after you graduate?" Ben asks out of nowhere.

"Is this a job interview?"

"It's a life interview." He grabs my hand, and I feel a rush of relief. It fits better there than it does anywhere else.

"I want to be a company member at Alvin Ailey." I can't remember the last time I let myself say that dream out loud. Maybe not since fourth grade.

"That's for sure gonna happen," Ben says. "Definitely. No doubt in my mind."

"Ben, you've never even seen me dance."

"But I've seen you walk. And I've seen you run across the street to make a light. And scoot around people who text on the subway stairs. You're a vision. I know you can do it."

"You make it sound so easy."

"It *is* easy. You're a hard worker and you're talented. You're doing all the right things. I know you'll make it to exactly where you want to be."

If only. I change the subject.

"What about you?" I ask.

"Yeah. Well, it's complicated, actually. I've waited my entire life to go to Brighton. I thought once I got there everyone else would be just like me and I'd finally understand why I have this deep fire inside me that never wants to burn out. But after two years I still don't feel like I fit in there. So many people at school are just content to get the notes right, and if they're in tempo, that's it — they're happy. But I have this — this thing inside me. Something else. I just know there has to be something more. And this is usually the part of the conversation where you're supposed to tell me I sound totally cocky and arrogant, and I'm supposed to get embarrassed and apologize, so I'm sorry."

"Don't be sorry. I think you're right."

"You do?"

"If you're not going to devote your whole heart, mind and body to a piece, what's the point of even doing it?"

"Exactly! Exactly. Art is worth giving up everything. If you want to stay safe, you're never going to be vulnerable enough to create something real. So that's it. That's my plan. To be vulnerable. To be real."

As we're walking, I can't help but wonder if his plan includes me. And then I realize something: until I'm vulnerable and real, it can't.

* *

We walk up to the green awning of Ben's building, and the doorman welcomes us in. The marble situation in the lobby is completely out of control. The floor is marble, the desk is marble, even the round containers that hold potted plants are marble. I can't help but wonder if the doorman would have given me the same treatment if I'd walked in alone. He has dark skin, too. Would he have glared and asked for my ID?

I'm hit with a jolt of nerves.

"Um, hey," I ask. "Do your parents know I'm coming up?"

"No. Why?"

"So they're okay with you just bringing a random girl upstairs to your apartment?"

"You're not some random girl. You're A Train."

"You know my actual name is Dom, right?"

"I know, A Train."

I smile. "Okay."

He presses the Up button outside the elevator, and after a few seconds the brass doors open. The elevator has an actual rug in it, like one of those maroon Persian rugs you'd see in a really nice doctor's office on TV. It's such a waste to have a carpet so nice in an elevator. I bet no one really even notices it.

We walk down a long hallway with more carpets and these little lamps with shades that stick right out of the wall. The place looks just like a hotel in a movie. It's quiet and clean and … I just can't believe people actually live here. That Ben actually lives here. I grab his hand again to try to get a little bit of that connection back, but he's so warm and my fingers are freezing. Our hands don't fit together the way they did outside.

Each door has a brass carved number, and a bunch of them have welcome mats in front, and some of them even have door knockers. My heart thunks as we walk to the very end of the hallway.

He turns his key in the door marked 1556 and we go inside.

For the first time everything is in color. Like when Dorothy opens her door into Oz.

There's a dark wooden coat rack to the left of the door, and Ben takes my jacket and hangs it on top of his. One of the walls is just a giant floor-to-ceiling bookcase. I'm not sure how anyone even reaches the books on top, but somehow the hardcover copies of *The Coast of Utopia* and *Writers at Work: The Paris Review Interviews* and *As I Lay Dying* don't look dusty at all.

Against the side wall is a long gray couch made of what looks like velvet, and just above that is an oil painting of an audience — like from the perspective of someone standing on a stage — with bright, shining lights and red seats. It's in this gigantic, carved frame that looks like it should be in a museum or something. If I squint hard enough, I can almost see Ben sitting in the crowd, watching *La Bohème* with his arm around me.

"Oh, that's from Rome," Ben says. "My dad had it commissioned by a local painter when I was playing in the youth orchestra at the Parco della Musica."

I take a step back and realize I'm totally out of my element. I feel like an imposter. Ben wants someone honest and vulnerable and real, like him. What am I doing here, in this sparkling-clean palace? He probably thinks I grew up like this. That my parents live in a five-bed-room house in Princeton with two cars and a pool. I swallow the guilt and make a mental note to tell him about the imaginary hot tub in our imaginary backyard.

It takes me a second to notice, but there's no TV anywhere. They can obviously afford one — they can probably afford a few hundred. Maybe there's a TV room somewhere else in the apartment. Or a screening room with a TV that takes up the entire wall.

In the corner of the room, by the window, there's a huge piano. And on the wall behind the piano there's a violin. I wonder how many concerts Ben has played in his life. Hundreds? Thousands?

There's a fireplace with a stone mantel, and a bunch of important-looking awards and plaques on it. I can see from across the room that most of them are Ben's. I look back over at him, and he's glancing at me out of the corner of his eye, like I'm doing something wrong.

"Dom, do you mind taking your shoes off? My mom is weird about getting footprints on the rug. I don't know if your mom is like that, if she just flips out over the smallest things. But if you could just take them off, it would make her very happy. Socks are fine, but shoes are forbidden."

"Sure," I say, and take them off. I squish my toes into the carpet and get the sense that even my bare feet aren't clean enough for this place.

The living room isn't that big, but judging by the sheer number of doors in it (four), the apartment could be gigantic. A weird feeling creeps up inside me again, a pins-and-needles feeling that I don't belong here. Ben's parents are going to walk in any second and they're going to see right through me, in my borrowed dress and my hand-me-down jacket, and they're going to wonder what the hell I'm doing with their brilliant son. In real life people like him don't fall in love with people like me.

Ben must notice I'm flipping out, because he puts his hand on my back. My breathing slows temporarily, and he leads me down the hallway.

"So my mom's a nurse and she's usually home on Saturdays, but she picked up an extra weekend shift, so she's probably at the hospital. My dad's a consultant for a hedge fund. I don't even know what that really means, to be honest. I mean, I know what a hedge fund is, but what is he consulting? Couldn't that mean pretty much anything? Why does he have to work every Saturday? When I was a kid, he would take me to auditions sometimes, but now it's like he's at the office consulting more than he's home. This is my brother, Milo's, room. And this is my dad's office, where he can come home after consulting and do more consulting. Bathroom's to your left. What does your dad do?"

"Huh?"

"What's his job?"

Professional eBay reseller? Couch refurbisher? Vendor of knock off purses? Odd-job guru? No. Instead I say, "He's a consultant, too."

"Oh, yeah? What firm?" he asks.

Damn it. "Hammersmith."

"I've never heard of that one."

"Oh, well, I'm sure there are millions." Hammersmith? Where the hell did that come from?

"So this is my room." He opens the door and we walk in. "It's nothing special. Just four slabs of painted drywall and a window, and then four more pieces of wood hammered together to make a bed, and four more to make a dresser, and —"

I grab his hand and realize it's trembling just as much as mine is.

He's nervous, too.

"I love it," I say.

It's the perfect room. It's just like a room in one of those sitcoms where the family has three kids and a golden retriever and all the clothes are folded and put away and every surface is sparkling clean. The carpet is cushy and I wish I could lie down and take a nap on it. I think about the threadbare rug in our living room with the duct tape spot where my mom patched up a hole.

I sit on the edge of his puffy comforter and he plays me songs on his fancy stereo system. First a couple of jazz songs. Then *La Bohème*. Then the *Kreutzer* Sonata, the new piece he's working on.

"I know I'm probably supposed to know this, but what is a sonata, exactly?" I ask him.

"Great question, A Train. It's a classical piece with one or more instruments. So for *Kreutzer*, which is one of Beethoven's most difficult violin sonatas, it's a violinist with a piano accompanist. There are three movements — uh, sections of the piece — and each one is totally different, and the violin and the piano take turns playing the melody. So first there's the allegro movement, and the theme of the sonata is being explored for the first time. It's a little frenetic and intense. Then when things begin to come together in the second movement, everything slows down. You'll hear the same things repeating again and again in the second movement, because Beethoven does this thing called 'theme and variations.' So he'll have an instrument play a theme, and then play it again a bunch of times with slight differences. And then there's the finale, presto. Basically, that's when the shit hits the fan. It's the fastest, craziest movement. It's basically like the end of a Fourth of July show when all the fireworks get set off at once."

He's talking a mile a minute and I can barely follow. "So basically, sonatas have a ton of rules," I say.

He snaps the music off and wipes his forehead with the back of his hand. "You know what? This is stressing me out. Let's listen to some jazz." He puts on Duke Ellington and we get lost in it together.

{28}

Ben

Before I knew her, there was a cavernous black hole inside me and I couldn't figure out why. Now, when she's with me, I'm still. I'm calm. Everything slows down and I can actually think. But my brain isn't filled with all my usual thoughts — worrying about how much more I need to practice and how much better I need to be. I'm just thinking about how lucky I am to be sitting here with her, listening to music on my bed as the world moves all around us.

The strangest thing is we didn't even kiss this time. I've kissed her before, so it's not like it would have been any big deal. But it's almost like sitting on the bed kissing Dom in total silence would be a waste of her. There's so much I want to ask her about and so many things I want to show her. I could sit in the dark with my eyes closed and kiss anyone. And don't get me wrong — I really, really want to with Dom. But with Dominique, you have to be slow and quiet and deliberate. You can't rush her. I would never want to rush her. Well, I'm so excited to be with her I never stop talking, so I probably end up rushing her, anyway. But there's something about her pace, like drips of honey, that I want to slow down for.

Like adagio sostenuto. At ease.

But now she's gone. It's back to reality, back to the empty apartment and back to *Kreutzer*. Alone, it's become painful. It's hardly music anymore, just a jumble of notes that hurt my ears.

It's never taken me so long to learn a piece before. Usually I play something a few times in the morning and I'm soaring through it by the afternoon. This one is tough, but it shouldn't be *this* tough. It's like I can't even trust myself anymore.

I try to listen one more time, then turn the recording off.

I need to schedule another rehearsal with Claire. That's the problem. We're not practicing together enough. That has to be it. I can't play a duet alone. I text her and wait for her to respond.

Robertson has to lose his mind when he hears us perform this, just like he did at Carnegie Hall. I've done it before. I can do it again. I just have to get it right.

I pull my violin out of its case and hold it under my chin as I grab my bow. There's one part of the third movement that's still not clicking, so I climb back in and hide there for the rest of the night. Trying to play the ache. Or is this piece causing the ache? I can't even tell anymore.

* *

"Ben, the kitchen's a mess. Could you come clean this up please?"

Mom in the doorway.

"Five minutes."

When I get to the end of the movement, I put down my violin. I come out and throw away Dom's granola-bar wrapper. I walk into the living room, and Mom is removing her coat and hanging it on the rack. She sighs, takes her hair down and combs through it with her fingers. I always forget how young she looks with her hair down. Like she could be in college.

"Did you have someone over?" she asks.

"Why?"

"The guest towels are all bunched up. You and Milo don't usually touch those."

"Yeah, I did."

"Who?"

"Just a friend from school."

I'm not sure why I don't tell my mom about Dominique. I guess I just want to keep her to myself. I know this is not something that can last forever — eventually Dom will have to meet my family — but not today. Today I want her to be mine.

"When you have friends over, make sure they use the towels on the bar by the sink."

"But aren't the guest towels for ... guests?"

"Not those kinds of guests. Thanksgiving guests. Passover guests."

"I don't understand the point of having something called a 'guest towel' if the guest can't even use them when she comes over. You can just throw them in the washing machine and clean them, can't you?"

"She?"

"Yeah."

She smirks and flops on the couch. "The first girl you've had over since Juliette."

I hate talking about this stuff with Mom. I change the subject. "How was your shift?"

She looks up at me with this strange expression, like she hasn't really heard me.

"What's wrong?" I say.

"You haven't asked me that in months."

"I haven't? That's not true. Every night you come home and you come into my room and I ask you how your day was. Don't I?"

"You don't."

"I'm sorry. I guess I've just been busy."

"It's okay, honey. I know you have a lot on your mind."

"Yeah."

"Yaz called yesterday to see how you were doing. Did you two have an argument?"

"Sort of."

"But you're feeling okay?"

"Yeah, I just lost my temper. I've never worked on a piece this hard before, and I guess I got frustrated. I'm fine."

"Do you want a bagel?"

"I'm okay."

We sit there for a minute, saying nothing. There's nothing to say.

{29}

Dominique

It's a nice night on Sunday, so I meet Cass on his stoop after helping Mom through most of the weekend laundry. He thinks we're just going to play the celebrity game and relax, but I can't. I need his advice.

"I can't do this," I say as I bound up the steps and sit down next to him.

"Can't do what?"

"I have to tell Ben the truth."

"What do you mean? It's been going great so far. He hasn't found out yet, right?"

"No, but he went on this whole thing after the opera about how important honesty is to him, and it's just making me feel terrible. I can't lie to him for one more second. I can't do it."

"Okay, I know you're feeling guilty, but I want you to really think this through. What if he gets upset? What if he never looks at you the same way again?"

My heart drops. It might mean that. There's a really, really good chance it might.

I have to be brave. I have to let myself be vulnerable.

"I need him to know. Even if it means losing him."

Cass shakes his head. "But this isn't supposed to happen until the end of the movie."

* *

After Mom closes up, she texts me and asks me to meet her at Adelia's Drugstore so we can pick up toilet paper and shampoo. The drugstore is an independently owned shop, and there really is an Adelia. She's in her eighties and too old to really work shifts now, but tonight, like most nights, she's sitting out front in her old white folding chair, doing a crossword puzzle. She waves to us and blows us a kiss as we walk in, and Mom and I wave back. Now her son, Carlos, and daughter, Paula, run the drugstore, and her grandkids work part-time after school, like I do. So many families came to Trenton with dreams of opening their own stores. So even though shopping here is a little bit more expensive than going down the street to the CVS Pharmacy, we try to support local businesses if we can. And they do the same for us. I just wish it were enough.

Mom puts a bottle of conditioner in her basket, adding up prices in her head, then roots through her purse for coupon combinations. She's been up since five. I don't know how she's even still standing. She's been working so hard, tirelessly, endlessly, for years, and makes only just enough to stay exactly where she is. Meanwhile Ben's parents can live in a huge, luxurious apartment with pristine white carpets and cushy couches and bookshelves. There's no way they work harder than my mom. So why isn't my mom the one who's rich? Isn't that the way things are supposed to be? If not, what's the point of working hard in the first place? I remember the $20 I took and get an awful feeling in my stomach. What kind of person steals from her own family business? Just for some stupid guy.

"Dom. Wake up." My mom is snapping her fingers in front of my nose.

"Huh?"

"I asked, 'Do you want lavender, vanilla or citrus?' "

"Surprise me," I say.

She throws a bottle of citrus-scented shampoo into the cart and we keep rolling down the aisle, fluorescent lights humming and flickering overhead.

I need to find a way to make the money back.

{ 3 0 }

Ben

Auditions for the Sonata Showcase are in two weeks and — surprise — Claire is avoiding me. I tried texting her again last night and she didn't respond. So I sent her an e-mail. Then another e-mail an hour later. Then I walked over to her building on West Sixty-Third Street and left a message with her doorman. Then I hung around outside for half an hour until the doorman came out and asked me if I needed help. I told him no, not unless he could help me get in touch with Claire. He told me he'd let me know as soon as she came home, then asked me to please stop standing in front of the building.

I spit on the sidewalk and walked away.

But I don't go home, because I can't sit still. It's like an itch that runs wild, covered in wool, and I can't predict when and why it happens. Dominique helps. But when she's not here, it claws the walls. It multiplies. It's itch on top of itch until I can't eat or sleep or breathe, and the only thing I can do is think about how I need to make it stop.

Stop.

If Claire isn't serious about our duet, we might as well not audition in the first place. I just wish she had the guts to tell me, instead of avoiding me like some coward. I've already devoted hundreds and hundreds of hours to this — I'm consumed, I can't even see straight. And she doesn't have one minute to text me back?

I'm ten blocks from Lincoln Center when the phone stops ringing. There's a click on the other line and then Claire's voice. I'm startled. Now that she's picked up I don't know what to say.

"What do you want, Ben?"

"We need to practice."

"I can't tonight."

"When can you?"

"Did it ever occur to you that maybe I have other classes? Other responsibilities? Other things going on besides you?"

"I have other things going on, too, but I'm willing to sacrifice my time because this is important to me."

"Let's talk about this after class tomorrow."

"That's an entire twenty-four hours of wasted time! Are you even working on your part? Ever since Robertson praised you, you've been acting like you're above all this. I hate to break it to you, Claire, but last time I checked, you're not Vladimir Horowitz. Not even close. You still need to practice like the rest of us."

"Ben, I didn't want to have to tell you this over the phone, but … I don't know what else to do."

"What are you talking about?"

"I don't want to do the showcase with you."

Blood bubbles up inside my brain, making my forehead hot and itchy. "What?"

"Yaz was going to tell you. Marie thinks it would be better if I paired up with Carter. He's been working on the first movement in his private lessons and … We played the piece together last week and it just clicked. His technique isn't as strong as yours and there's still a lot of work to do, but when we play together, it actually sounds like music."

"Are you fucking kidding me right now?"

"Please don't curse at me."

"When were you going to tell me?"

"Yaz was supposed to tell you this week. Ben, you've been acting so strange, and — I'm sorry. I didn't know what else to do. I —"

I hang up.

I'm speechless. I'm fucking speechless. This talentless nothing is trying to ruin my career because she's jealous? She's sabotaging everything I've ever worked for in my whole goddamn life, just like that. Oh, and she's been doing it for months, just dragging me along, toying with me, for fun. She must have been looking for an excuse to get me cut this whole time, so the missed classes and bad rehearsal with Robertson played right into her plan. Maybe she and Carter are having sex. They have to be. That's the only explanation. It can't be me. Everyone loves me. Everyone at school loves me.

The itch scatters, running over my body like trillions of spiders.

Don't they?

* *

Yaz's cell phone is going straight to voice mail. I call it again. Again. Again. He's probably having dinner at some fancy restaurant with his wife, drinking wine and eating steak. He's not thinking about me at all — he never is. He's not on my side, anyway. Robertson's on my side. He'll understand. He has to listen to me.

I run up the steps at Lincoln Center and race past the fountain, past the Performing Arts Library and the little rectangular pond with the trees next to it and up to Brighton's glass double doors. I push them open hard and they clatter. The receptionist looks surprised.

She narrows her eyes and raises her eyebrows. "Yes?"

"Dean Robertson has something important of mine," I say.

"Okay. And?"

"I need it back."

"I don't think any faculty members are still here, but I can leave —"

"No, I need to see him in person. I need his address."

"I'm sorry, but even if I had it, I'm not able to give out personal information to students."

"This is really, really important. Please."

"I'm sorry, but there isn't anything I can do."

"Please, I just need to pick up something from him."

"You're welcome to come back tomorrow morning — his first class is at eight." She glances at me with a glimmer of sympathy, like there's a chance she might give me his address after all. I keep trying.

"Listen, he has a priceless violin of mine. I took it to class and I'm so scatterbrained sometimes I must have left it behind, and I think he took it home to keep it safe, and now if I don't get it back, my parents are going to kill me. Like, literally murder me. I just need to know that it's safe. I'll just drop by, ring the buzzer and that will be it."

"I'm sorry."

"Well, then I'd like to reserve a practice room, please."

"What time?"

"From now until 8:00 a.m. tomorrow."

"You know I can't do that."

"Then I'll just stand here in the lobby."

The receptionist blinks. "Well, you're welcome to stay until the building closes at seven."

"This is my school. You can't tell me how long I can and can't stay."

"I'm sorry, but this building isn't open to students after 7:00 p.m. You're welcome to try —"

I bang my palm against the glass reception desk. "I need Robertson's address. Now."

A man in a security uniform steps out from the back room and leads me out the front door. He asks for my name, but I won't give it to him.

I'll just wait outside until Robertson gets here.

* *

My phone battery is at 12 percent, but I can't stop texting Dom. She's probably not even awake — she's not writing back. But I think of another place I want to take her. The Brooklyn Botanic Garden. There's this Japanese-inspired garden inside that I went to with my mom once when I was little. I was so bored at the time, and I remember grabbing my mom's sleeve and telling her I wanted to leave. But now I keep shutting my eyes and trying to transport myself back there. The flowering cherry trees. The little wooden shrine. The still, peaceful water.

This was back when Mom used to take me to auditions, before she trusted me to get on the train and go myself. I was auditioning for the California Conservatory summer program, which at the time felt like such a huge deal and now feels so small and silly. I didn't get in — I hadn't practiced enough and I botched a couple of notes, lost my place and had to start again. The judges said, "Thank you," but by the time I put my bow down I knew I hadn't been accepted. That day I realized that unless I worked my hardest to be better than everyone else, I'd never become a violinist. I'd be someone who sat in the audience.

Mom was upset because I was upset, and she thought that if we went to the Brooklyn Botanic Garden and looked at some trees, we'd both feel better. The air made me choke and the quiet made my mind race, and I felt worse instead of better. But now, maybe because I want to be anywhere but here, I wonder if it would help. I imagine sitting on a bench by the water with Dominique, her hand on my back.

I lean against the fountain. Luckily it's not freezing tonight. According to my phone, the low will be 52 degrees. That's manageable. I can handle that. Now my phone's only at 9 percent, but I put on *Kreutzer* anyway. My fingers are still. I don't play along. I just listen. I'm hearing both parts, not just my own. But Claire is still wrong about the pacing. It's not written into the music — she was slowing down.

My phone dies around half past three. Aside from a homeless man sleeping in the alcove near the Vivian Beaumont Theater stage door, I'm alone. Completely disconnected. I glance up at the sky. For the first time in I don't remember how long, I can see two stars cutting through the darkness just above my head. Clouds pass and they disappear.

A siren blares avenues away. Cabs drift by, looking for a fare. The streetlights turn green, then yellow, then red, then green again. Yellow. Red. Green. Yellow. Red. Green. Maybe none of it matters. Whether I'm out on the street or at home, or if I end up headlining a concert in Prague when I'm twenty-five or I go tie myself to the subway tracks with violin strings right now, it's all the same. It all goes on.

Yellow. Red. Green. Yellow. Red. Green.

If I'm not the best violinist at Brighton, who am I?

Nobody.

* *

Robertson rushes past the fountain, paper coffee cup in hand. I'd tell you what time it is, but I have no idea. It's light out, and some students have already gone in to practice, so I'd guess it's somewhere between 7:00 and 7:45.

I chase after him, which isn't hard because I've been running around the perimeter of the fountain for the last two hours. At first I was just trying to beat my record of 5.3 seconds, and then I started trying to see how far I could run, like how many miles I could log just running around the same cement circle over and over and over. I lost count at 354 rotations and was too dizzy to figure out the perimeter of the fountain and calculate the total distance. But the point is I'm totally warmed up, ready to chase Robertson across the entire campus if I have to.

"Dean Robertson, wait. Hey, Dean Robertson —"

He turns and sees me just as he reaches the glass doors. There's an initial beat of recognition, and then there's an additional beat of shock, like he didn't expect to see me here this early. I run up to meet him, but he takes a step back.

"You're soaked, Ben. Is everything okay?"

"Claire told me she's auditioning for the Sonata Showcase with Carter now."

"Have you spoken with Yaz?"

"It's not fair to tell someone you're going to work on a piece with them and then leave that person completely out of the loop while you rehearse with someone else. What the hell is that?"

"It sounds like she didn't handle it properly. But if not the Sonata Showcase, there will be lots of opportunities for you here. There's an incredible violin solo in —"

"What about Carnegie Hall? You told me I have what it takes to be one of the best violinists in the world. Why the hell would she pick Carter over me? Just between us, Dean Robertson, he's really been struggling recently. He barely got through the Mendelssohn concerto. He'll butcher *Kreutzer* and he'll bring Claire down with him. His technique is all off. He rushes. His vibrato is all over the place. I don't understand why no one else sees that. Why can't anyone else actually listen? He's not even playing music. You told me I was amazing. So why am I the one being punished?"

I wait for him to reassure me. To give me some advice, something.

Instead Robertson takes a sip of his coffee and stares at me.

"What?" I ask. "Am I not talented? Do I not belong here? Someone please just tell me. I'm begging you. Please."

He takes another sip of his coffee.

"Yes, you have to be the best to get into this school," he says at last. "You're a supremely talented violinist — you know that. But it's your inconsistency I'm worried about. You and Yaz have discussed this at length. You missed your Queen Elizabeth audition, and then those ... issues with Professor Nadelstein began to surface. You took a break, you got some rest, and there isn't any shame in that. Over the last few months you've seemed more focused, and you had an amazing concert at Carnegie Hall. That's wonderful. But your work since then has been hit-or-miss. Technically, you're astounding. But this isn't healthy, Ben. I need to look out for your well-being and that of every other student at this school, so it's time for me to step in here."

"She's just jealous — that's all this is. She's upset at me because I've been dating this girl, and she's been acting strange ever since. I guess she's just been in love with me for all these years. But I shouldn't be punished because she can't handle rejection. And she is definitely sleeping with Carter, by the way."

"You and Claire have two different versions of this story."

"If you think I'm so supremely talented, just convince her to work with me. We've come so far. She can't just decide to start working with someone else one day and not even tell me. What the fuck is her problem?"

"Ben, please remember what we agreed on after your probation."

"This has nothing to do with that. I haven't gone anywhere near Isaac Nadelstein or his apartment in six months — well, one time we were on the elevator together, but that was an accident. I saw the therapist for the prescribed two months, I'm going to class, I'm practicing, my performances are incredible, I'll be ready to audition for competitions again this season — what else could you people possibly want from me?"

My whole face is wet and stinging. I can't tell if it's sweat or tears.

"Claire has asked to work with Carter because she no longer feels comfortable working with you."

"What? Why?"

"I'd like to schedule a meeting with you, Yaz and your parents as soon as possible so we can discuss this in detail," he says. "I've left a few messages for your mother and haven't heard anything back. Will you —"

"But why? Please. What did I do wrong?"

Robertson wipes his forehead with his shirt cuff. I'm making *him* nervous for once, instead of the other way around. My lips curl up into an involuntary smile. I can't help it.

"Claire told me you've been calling her obsessively," he says at last. "Going to her apartment unannounced. Her doorman reported a person who fits your description standing outside her building for three hours."

"It wasn't three hours."

"But it was you."

"Yeah."

"Ben."

"I just want us to be the best."

"I know you do. But this is a problem. You have a problem."

"But I have the opening. I can play it in my sleep. It sounds as good as it does on the Nadelstein recording — better. Whatever you were hearing at the rehearsal, whatever is making her doubt me, it's not me, it's not my playing. Maybe it's my strings. Maybe if I restring the E and try something a little different, everything will click. Just let me try it one more time. Let me play for you again."

"Don't worry about coming to the rest of your classes today. I'll give you an excused absence. Go home and get into some dry clothes."

I look down. My clothing is soaked all the way through. Even my jacket. Like I spent the whole night swimming in the fountain.

He puts his hand on my shoulder. "Get some sleep, okay? I'll try your parents again. We'll sort this out."

"Okay," I say, even though I don't believe him.

It's weird. You think I'd storm off, or start crying or yelling, or kick the side of the fountain. Instead I shake my head and laugh. I laugh all the way down the stairs, all the way to Lexington Avenue. I'm laughing so hard I can't stop.

{31}

Dominique

I start with the easiest stuff first. Slowly, like easing into a frigid swimming pool. I don't want to involve Cass in this, so I sneak into the library during lunch to use the computer.

To: lookingforatrain@gmail.com
From: hidingbehindcurls@gmail.com
Subject: Confession
October 15, 12:46 p.m.
Ben. Hi. What I'm about to say is really, really tough for me ... but you deserve the truth. So I'm just going to type it out as fast as I can, before I change my mind, okay?

I haven't been entirely honest with you. Actually, I haven't been honest about anything. You know when we first met at the fountain, when I asked you for directions? Well, I'd actually seen you before, performing at Carnegie Hall. I almost came up to you then, but I didn't have the guts. You were so amazing I just couldn't bring myself to do it. So I tracked you down and pretended I was lost so you'd talk to me. You just seemed so wonderful and brilliant and kind I got swept up in the whole thing. You asked me if I went to NYU and I just said yes. I didn't know what else to do. I wasn't thinking. And then it kind of spiraled out of control from there.

So, the truth. I'm still in high school. I'm seventeen. I live in Trenton, New Jersey, in a not-great part of town. My mom owns a laundromat and my dad isn't a consultant. I don't know why I told you that. I don't even really know him. He left when I was little and I've seen him, like, four times since then. All I know is that he's Ecuadorian, he lives in Spanish Harlem and I can't remember the last time he paid child support. My mom works twice as hard to make up for it, but it's never enough. God, I want you to meet her. She's amazing. She's like a superhero. My dad, on the other hand … some days I wish I could go to his apartment and punch him in the face.

I don't know why I did this. I just wanted you to like me, I guess. I wanted to be a part of your life. I *wanted* your life, and everything beautiful and magical that came with it. When I'm with you, it's like all the wonderful stuff, all the art and love and music, floats up to the surface. And all the terrible things sink to the bottom. You make me feel like I'm deserving of happiness. So that's why I haven't told you the truth. But we're in too deep now. And you deserve to know every part of me. Even the things I'm ashamed of.

So if you never want to talk to me again, I understand. It would kill me, but I deserve it. I'm so, so sorry for lying. I just couldn't go another minute without telling you. I'm sorry.

Love, Dominique

The rest of the day is complete and total torture, as I wait for him to respond.

Nothing after geography.

Nothing after music.

Nothing after study hall.

Nothing, nothing, nothing.

* *

Before I leave school, I check my e-mail one more time. Nope. Still nothing. That's it.

Ben probably doesn't want to date someone who would lie to him. He probably thinks honesty is the most important thing in the world — which maybe it is — and he's wondering if he should go out with me at all. If I'm worth his time.

He'll probably never speak to me again.

I walk past Smokers' Corner and there's good old reliable Anton, sucking on an e-cig with Raf and his stupid friends. They spot me immediately, and I look down at the pavement, trying to pretend I don't see them.

"Baby," Raf yells across the crowd.

I don't answer.

"Hey, baby, Anton has something to tell you."

Then his voice takes a gruff tone that makes my stomach flip.

"You answer me when I'm talking to you."

I walk right past them without even looking up. They don't have power over me anymore.

Behind me I can hear Anton: "Leave her alone," he says. "She's not worth it."

Whoa. In his stupid jerk way, he's actually kind of sticking up for me. Maybe because I told him off, he's actually starting to respect me.

About damn time.

I keep walking and don't look back.

* *

When I walk into Spin Cycle, Mom has her calculator and a bunch of receipts on the counter. She's looking down, and I don't think she even notices me. My stomach lurches. I already know what she's doing.

"Hi, Mom."

"Hi, honey. Can you come over here and add up these numbers for me?"

I go up to the counter and enter each receipt into the calculator.

"Okay, now count the money in here."

I wipe my hands on my jeans and count the bills in the blue zipper bag, knowing the cash is going to turn up $20 short.

"Uh, $560," I say. "What did you get?"

"Same — $560. It's supposed to be $580."

"Could the bag have fallen? Maybe some money slipped between the wall and the counter?" I get down on my hands and knees and feel around on the floor, behind the dusty cords of the cash register. Of course nothing's there.

"We need to get a better system. Something electronic, where we can put in our earnings every night so we don't have this problem."

"Okay, that sounds good," I say. My face is burning and I'm afraid to get back up from under the counter. I know she'll be able to tell I'm lying.

"From now on, every night before you leave, I want you to count the register and make sure we're on track, and I'll do the same thing before I close up."

"Definitely."

"Do you think you could have been making change for a fifty and two twenties were stuck together?"

"It's possible."

"What?"

"It's possible," I say a little louder.

"I can't hear anything you're saying. Can you come back up here?"

Shit. I wipe my eyes and edge out from under the table, hitting my head in the process.

"What did you say?" she asks again.

"I said that it's possible."

"Well, we need to make sure there's no possibility of that happening. No margin of error. I don't understand — we've only ever been a few pennies short before. How could we be missing a twenty?"

I didn't realize she'd be so worked up about it. For some reason I thought she would assume we'd made a mistake, wonder what happened for a few minutes and then let it go. I know money is tight, but I didn't realize $20 was so crucial. It's so hard to watch her pacing the store, back and forth. I should never have done this. My throat feels full of cotton and I want to cry.

"Mom," I say. My voice comes out all trembly, even though I'm mentally willing it not to. "I'm sorry. I think I did make change for a fifty the other day, and maybe two of the bills were stuck together like you said. I remember now. I'm so sorry."

She stops pacing and her face softens. "It's okay, baby. But you have to be more careful next time. We both will."

She hugs me and I squeeze back, hard. I'm not sad or embarrassed — I'm mostly relieved that I wasn't caught. I wonder what that says about me. Am I a terrible person?

I'm pretty sure I'm a terrible person.

* *

I call Cass on my way home.

"Hey," I say. "Did I wake you up?"

"No, just watching *The Red Shoes*. You ever see that one?"

"I don't think so."

"Oh, my gosh, you have to. It's about this ballerina in London who —"

"Cass, I sent Ben my confession."

"When?"

"At lunch."

"And?"

"And he hasn't responded yet."

"Maybe he's just busy."

"Or maybe he decided he doesn't like me after all."

"I don't see how that's possible. You told him the truth. There's nothing braver and more beautiful than that."

"Is that from a movie?"

"Nope, that's just me."

"Love you."

"Love you, too. Don't stress, okay?"

"Okay." Talking to Cass makes me feel a little better, and I can take a deep breath again. Ben's probably just busy. He's probably working on a school project or stuck late at rehearsal.

"Goodnight, babe."

"Goodnight."

{32}

Ben

The resonance is off. There's this buzzing. Like a gnat in my ear whenever I press down on the E string. I've tried retuning, then restringing, then putting on a different string. Then another. Nothing helps. It's like every phrase comes out sounding thin and shrill, like I'm listening to someone else. Someone with completely shitty tone quality who has no idea what he's doing. Someone like Carter.

The phone rings in my ear. I tap my fingers on my desk, first in eighth notes, then sixteenths, then thirty-seconds. I hold my breath until I hear the click.

"Virtuoso."

"Fred?"

"Hi again, Ben. What's up?"

"What if I put in a silver-wound G?"

"You tried that a few years ago, remember? You didn't like how bright it sounded."

"I want to try it again."

"Isn't the problem the E?"

"Yeah, but now I'm wondering if it's the discrepancy between the sound of the G and the sound of the E that's bothering me. Maybe the E is bothering me because the G is off. Does that make sense?"

He sighs. "Have you already opened everything you bought yesterday? I can only do an exchange if the packages are sealed."

"I'm just going to come by and get a few more. I want to swap them out and hear them against each other. Be there in fifteen minutes."

"We'll be here."

I'm playing all the same notes, but nothing sounds like it should. There's something whining and grating and piercing about the sound when I play, but I can't figure out why. It has to be the strings. I take impeccable care of my instruments. When we bought my Mezzadri, Yaz made sure my parents had humidifiers installed in our house to keep everything at the optimum 30 percent humidity. My case has a small humidifier inside to keep the wood from warping. I just had the fingerboard replaced a few months ago. There's no reason the sound should be so repulsive. It has to be the strings. There's no other possible explanation.

Unless it's me.

No. I stick the old strings in my closet and go into the living room. I put on my shoes and yank the laces, tying them tight. Tighter, tighter, tighter, until my feet feel like shrink-wrapped sausages. I imagine walking with my sausage feet all the way to the music store, then loosen the laces a bit. I tear out of the lobby and make the familiar trip to Virtuoso — the same one I made yesterday and the day before and the day before that.

* *

I'm back in my room, restringing, when Milo comes in. Not just the E and the G. I've decided I need to try several different brands and types of strings and listen to the tone of each setup back-to-back.

"Can't you even knock?" I say, not looking up.

"I've been knocking for like three minutes. You didn't hear me?"

"What?"

"Do you want lunch or something?"

"No."

"It's four-thirty. Mom asked me to come in. She wants to know if you want a sandwich. Cucumber and hummus with peppers. She told me to make it sound really delicious."

"If Mom wants me to eat lunch, she should ask me herself."

Before I can realize what's happening, Milo grabs my arms — each nerve ending on my skin is a shorting-out wire, alive and flashing. I wince and try to pull away, but he doesn't let go.

"Why are you so mean to us?"

He yells right in my face. Like I'm a toddler. Like I'm five years old.

"Why won't you just leave me the fuck alone?" I yell back.

"Is that what you want? You just want all of us to ignore you, like you're some brilliant composer here in his private wing and we're just your servants, bringing you food and making sure you've slept and tending to you like you're the goddamn king of the world?"

"That's not fair. I'm ..."

"You're what?"

"I'm ..."

The groaning of the room is so loud I can't hear myself finish the sentence. The ceiling shifts and it's a high E. An ambulance siren blares through the open window, a whining tritone. Milo's feet shuffling on the carpet become syncopated eighth notes. The sounds are all whirling together, picking up more and more speed in my mind until I begin to see the notes in my vision, too. Jumbled sixteenth notes fly in through the window and hover over the bed for a minute before raining down onto my comforter.

"Ben? Are you okay? Do you want me to get Mom?"

I put my hands on his shoulders. Wet, gripping. "Please, please leave me alone."

"Okay," he says softly. He pulls away and shuts the door with a D-flat thud.

My room is quiet and still again. The notes disappear.

I'm better when I'm alone. Milo and my mom think they know what's good for me, but they're only making things worse. They're just two more obstacles holding me back from who I could really be. I can't let them stand in my way anymore.

Back to the strings. None of these sound right. Not the gold-plated Olives, not the Gold Label E, not the synthetic Obligatos, not anything. Could it be the violin itself? Maybe the air went off in the apartment one day when no one was home and it got too warm and something warped. Maybe I'm not noticing a crack in the body. Maybe the sound post moved. Or maybe it's the bow. I've been playing with a Hill bow for the last five years, just like Isaac Nadelstein. I peel off my sweat-drenched T-shirt and put on a clean one, first inside out and backward, then the right way. Maybe I should try playing a Gagliano or a Guadagnini or a Guarneri, or maybe I should just go down to Brighton's rare-instruments room and play them all, every single one of them until I find the one that has the most perfect tone. Or just fucking buy a Stradivarius and stay in debt for the rest of my life.

I run to Virtuoso, ignoring Don't Walk signs, shrieking tires, screaming horns. Nothing else in the world matters.

* *

Just as the sun starts to set behind the Empire State Building, my mind sputters and shorts. Slowly, then all at once, like stumbling off a jagged cliff into nothing. My brain tries to fight it. Not yet, not yet

— I have so much to do, don't you understand? But a deeper part of me knows I could never go on like this. It always ends.

Somehow I get home.

I crawl to the safe cocoon of my room.

Sleep comes for me.

I am nowhere.

{33}

Dominique

He has to respond today. It's been forty-eight hours. He can't give me the silent treatment forever.

The day trudges on. Classes wash over me. I fold clothes at Spin Cycle: One sleeve, then the next, then up the center, then into the pile. I sleep in my clothes. I startle awake and run into the living room to check my e-mail, breath caught in my throat … then barreling into my stomach when I see that he still hasn't responded. I repeat it all the next day and the next. But nothing.

Nothing matters if Ben has given up on me.

{ 3 4 }

Ben

I can't move my leg. It's twisted around something wet, and I'm both cold and hot at the same time. I look up and see I'm caught in the bedsheet, which is pinning me to the mattress like the world's least practical toga. I'm not sure how my clothes came off. I must have ripped them off in my sleep.

My tongue is made of dog fur. My nose is packed with sand. My eyelids have splinters. It's too bright to blink — shutting them is easier.

* *

Something cold and wet presses into my forehead. I open my eyes and see Mom sitting beside me, holding a washcloth on my forehead. I'm wearing pajamas and the blankets are pulled up around my neck.

"You're burning up," Mom says. "Do you think you have the flu?"

I nod — not because I think I do but because words are too hard.

"How about staying home?"

I nod.

"I'll call Yaz and tell him you're not feeling well."

I shut my eyes.

Her footsteps fade into the hallway and the door clicks. Then there's nothing again.

* *

Mom is sitting on my bed with a bowl of pasta. Immediately I know it's from Upland — my favorite restaurant in the city.

All at once I'm painfully hungry, like all the missed meals from the last few weeks have hollowed out my stomach and now it's just an insatiable black hole. I can't cram pasta into my mouth fast enough. I can't even taste it. I'm just swallowing as fast as I can force it in. Mom pats my leg, makes a little hiccupy sighing sound, then turns away to wipe her eyes.

The bowl is empty, so I roll over. A few minutes later Mom leaves with the empty dishes. I briefly think about reaching over and grabbing my phone off the nightstand. I'm sure I have a million texts and e-mails. I'm sure everyone at school is worried. Or maybe no one cares. Maybe no one even noticed I was gone. Claire and Carter are probably at her house, running the second movement right now. And then I remember Dominique. Would she even want to talk to me if I didn't go to Brighton?

I shut my eyes. It aches too much to do anything else.

{35}

Dominique

I can't take it anymore. I skip chemistry and peek into the window of Cass's English class. Thankfully Ms. Arrojo's back is to me, so I wave wildly and hope Cass notices. When he does, I motion for him to meet me outside.

He opens the door and walks out with the bathroom pass, looking annoyed.

"We're about to have a pop quiz," he tells me. "I had to pretend I was going to pee my pants. This better be good."

"I can't take this anymore. I need to see Ben. If he hates me, I need him to tell me to my face. I can't just keep wondering. This is going to drive me insane."

"Okay, so tomorrow after school you can —"

"I can't wait until tomorrow. I need to talk to him now. There's a twelve-fifteen train. Maybe I can catch him when he's switching classes. He has music theory on Wednesdays and then he has to go uptown to get to his private lesson."

"Dom, you know I support you in everything you do."

"Yeah."

"But I'm not getting good vibes from Ben right now. I think you should just leave him alone until he cools off. If he wants to call you, he can. The ball is in his court. Just try to distract yourself," he says.

"I can't." I feel the tears dripping down my cheeks and onto my neck. "I don't know what's happening to me. I can't think about anything else. If he treats me like I don't exist, it's like I'm not even here." I can barely put words to the emptiness.

"Okay, here's what I want you to do. Wait an hour. And if you still feel like you're going to explode, then go for it. Here." He hands me a twenty from his wallet. "Baby-sat my cousins last week."

I grab him as tight as I can. "Thank you, thank you, thank you," I whisper into his shoulder.

"Just don't get caught. You know which door to use?"

"Yeah."

Anton and I used to do it all the time. Wait until the late bell, when all the classroom doors are closed. Walk around the back way, past the cafeteria and down to the dead end where the utility closets are. Leave out the door marked "Emergency Exit: Warning — alarm will sound." (This is a lie. There's not even an alarm connected to the door.)

I open the door and a high-pitched siren squeals.

Shit. Maybe the alarm got fixed.

Running is the only thing I can think to do. So I run. I run like a freaking track star. I run like an Olympic gold medalist. I run until my legs are numb and rubbery and my lungs are filled with a thousand needles. I don't stop running until I reach the train platform. Trenton to New York City.

* *

It's freezing outside, so the fountain is empty today. I watch students with instrument cases scurry back and forth across the stone tiles of the plaza at Lincoln Center — guess they're too cold to walk at a normal pace. I wish I had a heavier jacket.

Darkness creeps in and the lights outside Alice Tully Hall switch on. I walk down the steps and into the frenzy of rush hour. He's not here.

* *

It takes me a while to find his apartment building. I know he lives on Ninety-Sixth Street, but I can't remember if he's at Madison or Park or Lexington. Why do those avenues have to be so confusing? Why couldn't they stay a part of the number system like the streets?

I wander up Lexington and finally spot his building, with the green awning and the marble lobby. When I find it, I can't believe I ever even forgot where it was. A force larger than I am is drawing me there. I take a deep breath and push open the glass door.

"Hello," the doorman says cheerfully.

"Hi," I say.

"Can I help you?"

"Yes, I'm looking for Ben Tristan."

"Is he expecting you?"

"No."

"May I have your name?"

"Dominique."

"Your last name, Dominique?"

"Dominique Hall."

"Just a moment, Ms. Hall."

He has a faint, familiar-sounding accent. I have the urge to ask if he's from Ecuador. But I don't.

He picks up an old-school phone, presses a few buttons, then speaks into the receiver: "A young lady named Dominique Hall is here to see Mr. Ben."

He must be talking to one of Ben's parents. For some reason I thought Ben would be alone, like the last time we were at his apartment together. It didn't even occur to me that his mom — or God, his entire family — would be there, too.

"You know what? I just realized I can talk to him tomorrow," I tell the doorman. "Never mind."

"Mrs. Tristan said to go right up. Fifteenth floor, apartment 1556."

"Oh. Okay."

He gestures to the elevator.

Numb, I stumble over and press the button. Why am I doing this? Cass is right. If Ben doesn't want to see me, that's his decision. He's not going to change his mind just because I'm here.

But then, before I can stop myself, I'm upstairs, ringing his doorbell. What if I just turned around and went back down? It's too late; the elevator would never come in time and they'd see me standing there. What if I took the stairs? There have to be stairs somewhere, for emergencies. There have to be —

A blond woman opens the door. She's wearing a gray sweater and white jeans, just like a mom on the cover of a Macy's catalogue. Here she is in the flesh, a mother-on-paper.

"Come in, come in," she says.

Like she knows exactly who I am.

I step into the beautiful sanctuary once again, which is somehow even cleaner than last time. It's more quiet and peaceful than I've ever imagined a home could be.

"Hi," I sputter.

"Thank you so much for coming. I'm starting to wonder if it's mono. Is there something going around school?"

"Uh —"

"Do you have his schoolwork? He hasn't even picked up his violin in three days, which is so unlike him. Usually he's in his room playing away, right through colds, the flu, everything, determined to stay ahead. He had pneumonia once, a 102-degree fever and almost had to go to the hospital, but there he was, up at seven and practicing." She smiles apologetically. "Well, you know Ben."

I smile, too. Now I know where Ben gets the "talking too much" gene.

"Can I see him?" I ask.

"That's very sweet, love — what did you say your name was?"

"Oh. Sharon."

"I wouldn't want you to catch anything, Sharon. But I'll tell him you stopped by and asked about him, of course. Do you have the schoolwork?"

Should I make some up? I could ask to borrow some paper and an envelope and write a note to Ben, begging him to forgive me. And stuff it inside the envelope and lick the seal and press it shut. And say it's an assignment that only Ben can see.

Instead I look at the carpet and say, "Tell him to read pages 110 to 125 of his music composition textbook."

"And did you bring the assignments?"

I rummage through my backpack, knowing I have nothing to give her.

"You know what?" I say. "I must have left the packet at home. I'm so sorry. Just tell him to keep watching the list of videos I sent him last week, and I'll e-mail him the rest."

I back out of the apartment, hands shaking. Everything shaking. Mrs. Tristan looks confused but waves, says goodbye and that it was nice to meet me (well, not me but Sharon). She shuts the door.

I don't breathe until I'm safe inside the elevator. Somewhere around the third floor my heart settles back into my rib cage. So Ben has mono. Unless he's pretending to be sick to avoid me.

I can't believe I'm even thinking that. Of course he has mono. No wonder he hasn't responded. It's all perfectly understandable.

Still, he could text and tell me what's going on. Or send an e-mail. Unless he's in the hospital, unconscious, there's really no reason he wouldn't. He'd never want me to worry — would he?

The more days pass, the more I don't know.

{ 3 6 }

Ben

There's a crack in the corner of the ceiling. It looks like a lobster claw. Soft curves on the outside and jagged edges in the middle.

Just breathing feels like torture. It takes up all the energy I have.

There's a water stain above my head. I imagine rain falling on the roof, dripping through the ceiling and then pouring onto my face. I take a deep breath, as big as I can, and suck in every drop of water until the room is dry. My lungs are wet and sloshing inside me, soaking up every last water molecule like a sponge until I can't breathe anymore.

Sleep comes again.

{37}

Dominique

On the eighth day I give up hope. We'll never talk again. It meant nothing to him. I bet he goes on dates with different girls every week. He's probably been to the Village Vanguard three times since he took me. I was nothing special. I am nothing special.

{38}
Ben

{39}

Dominique

I've started skipping lunch and going to the library instead. The noise of three hundred kids all yelling and laughing at once and the greenish fluorescent lights and the old-tire lunch meat smell are too much to handle right now. I have a routine: I grab a dance book from the nonfiction section, hole up in a computer station and read while checking my e-mail for messages from Ben.

But today I break the routine. I don't even bother to check. The disappointment hurts too much. I know nothing is there.

{ 4 0 }

Ben

On Thursday morning things start to make sense again. I'll go over to Yaz's and see if I can try some of his violins. He'll tell me the truth. He doesn't sugarcoat anything. He'll tell me what I really sound like. I still feel like shit, but at least I have a plan. A reason to wake up.

In bed I hug my knees to my chest, trying not to cry. I'm normal. Everything's normal. I'm here. I'm okay.

I take my phone off the nightstand and try to turn it on, but the battery is dead. I can't remember the last time I checked it. Two, maybe three days ago? I stumble over to the desk and plug it in. There are texts from Amy and Kelly saying they hope I feel better. "Mono suuuuuucks" Jun-Yi writes with a thousand *u*'s stretched across the screen. The texts go all the way back to last Monday. Has it really been that long? And why does she think I have mono?

Then I check my e-mail. And there's one from Dominique.

I read it. Shit. Why didn't she feel she could be honest with me from the beginning? I never would have judged her. She's the most glorious human in the universe. Why would I care if she doesn't actually go to NYU? What a stupid thing to lie about.

Actually, she lied about everything.

Do I even know this girl anymore? Did I even know her at all?

And then it hits me. I haven't been honest with her, either. She thinks I'm the best violinist at Brighton. She thinks I'm on track to becoming the next Joshua Bell. She probably thinks she'll spend her life staying in four-star hotels and traveling the world with me. If she only had any idea how far from the truth that is. No one at school wants to work with me anymore. They're afraid of me. Who am I to be upset with her, when I can't even face the truth about myself?

* *

I pull on an undershirt and wander into the living room. Milo is there, playing some video game I've never seen before, where you have to shoot these weird alien pirates who are invading a ghost ship in the middle of the ocean.

"What day is it?" I ask.

Milo puts the game on Pause. "Why, Ebenezer, it's Christmas Day."

"Shut up. Is it Thursday?"

"Yeah, 6:36 on Thursday."

"In the morning or at night?"

"Jesus. Night. You were really zonked out."

"Yeah."

"Mom's been telling people it's mono."

"Huh."

"It's not mono, is it?"

"What's that supposed to mean?"

"Exactly what you think it means."

"Well, I don't know what it was, but I have to go over to Yaz's and try some of his violins. Something's wrong with my E string."

"So you're … fine now? That's it? That's all you're going to say?"

"I hate to disappoint you, but yes. See you later."

"If you go to Yaz's right now, Mom's literally going to murder me. She canceled my tennis lesson and gave me fifty bucks so I would sit here for two hours and then bring you a bowl of pasta at seven."

"She's being ridiculous. I don't need you to babysit me."

"Ben."

He narrows his eyes and gets really serious. I don't know what his problem is.

"What?"

"I saw inside your closet."

Milo looks down. He's afraid to look at me.

"Who the hell told you to go in there?"

"I wasn't snooping. Mom asked me to find your robe and … I didn't say anything to her and she hasn't seen it. Just … Ben, why did you do that?"

"It's not a big deal."

"How much money did you spend?"

"You have no idea what you're talking about. You have no fucking idea."

"Well, you're sure not making it very easy for me to figure out. Do you know how worried Mom and Dad were this week? Mom spent half the night in there with you. She's working a double right now, probably after getting four hours of sleep for the last eight nights. Not like that's a big deal to you. You're just a robot who does the same thing every day until, all of a sudden, you just crash."

"I was sick!"

"When I get the flu, I sit in bed and blow my nose a lot."

"This is mono. It's completely different from the flu."

"You weren't tested. She didn't even take you to the doctor. She's a nurse, for God's sake, and she's in as much denial as you are. She just wants it to be mono because she's sunk so many hours and so much money into your music career at this point that it would ruin her life if this didn't work out. She can't face the fact that her son isn't just an eccentric musician but actually has something wrong with him. Seriously wrong. I'm sorry, but I'm sick of everyone tiptoeing around you, treating you like you're some kind of fragile genius who can't be disturbed. You're not just stressed about learning this piece. This is something else entirely."

"Well, by all means, Milo, expert on everything. Tell me. What the fuck is wrong with me?"

"Something's off, Ben. Mentally. This kind of stuff keeps happening, and it's getting worse and worse every time. I don't know if it's depression or OCD or —"

I scream, grab the game controller out of his hand and throw it against the wall as hard as I can. It makes the world's most satisfying smash. Fortissimo.

I don't need this. I don't fucking need this. I'm leaving. Until the damp, cool air in the hallway washes over me, I didn't realize how hot and stifling it was in the apartment. In the elevator I text Yaz and tell him I'm coming over.

I'm halfway to Yaz's before I realize I'm only wearing an undershirt.

{ 4 1 }

Dominique

Cass and I are walking to Spin Cycle after school, playing the celebrity game. It used to feel like a secret escape from our real lives, but now it just feels pathetic and sad. The same old actors over and over again. Nothing ever happens and no one ever wins.

"Jackie Gleason," Cass says.

"Gene Kelly," I say.

"Always with Gene Kelly. I'm going to ban him from all future rounds."

"Fine, Greta Garbo. And you can't use Gene Kelly, either."

"Damn it."

"Do you want a hint?" My phone buzzes in my pocket. It's probably my mom, wondering if I can pick something up on my way over. "Hang on."

But it's him.

VIOLIN BOY BEN
Meet me at corner of 20th and Irving
at 9:00 a.m. on Saturday, *mi amor.*
Dancing shoes mandatory.

Tiny earthquakes run up my fingertips. Everything's trembling. *Mi amor.* My love. He loves me. In Spanish.

"I have to sit down."

"What?" Cass asks, grabbing my shoulders. "What is it?"

"He texted."

"About time."

I sit down on a stoop in front of a bodega. Cass squeezes in next to me.

Should I be mad? After ten days of the silent treatment, he's expecting me to drop everything and meet him at the corner of Twentieth and Irving, like it's nothing? What the hell happened? Is he okay? I thought he'd written me off. I thought he didn't want anything to do with me. I thought he was gone forever.

And then all the old stress flies back. What kind of dancing shoes is he talking about? I can't wear my real ones outside — they'll get ruined. And what outfit do I wear? I'll have to borrow something else. Another dress. But Monica's mom hasn't dropped off any clothes this week.

For a minute I think I should ignore his text like he ignored me, but I can't. Now, after Ben, my old life doesn't fit. It's like I was putting on the same black shirt every day for the last seventeen years and then one morning I woke up and put on a bright gold one and realized the black one was way too tight and completely the wrong color. I just never noticed before.

* *

"Dominique! *¿Cómo estás? ¡Tanto tiempo!*"

"Still *no habla español*, Rico."

I'm standing at checkout aisle three at Dollar Plenty, where Rico, the assistant manager, is manning the register in a red vest. On the front pocket, his vest says "Got a dollar? Then you've got plenty" — a slogan I recognized as terrible even when Mom used to work shifts here when I was five.

"How's your mama? Haven't seen her in a long time."

"Still running the laundromat."

"When is she going to ditch that old shack and come back to work for us? Have you seen that giant new place on Route 1? It's like Disneyland."

"Actually, that's why I'm here. I was wondering if, um, you have any shifts available."

"For your mom?"

"No, for me. Not, like, a full-time thing, but maybe a few hours after school a few times a week?"

"Instead of the laundromat?"

"No, in addition. Just to have a little more spending money."

"Does your mom know you're over here?"

"Not exactly."

"What if I called her right now? You think she'd be cool with this?"

I put my hand on his arm. "Please don't." Then I realize I don't know this guy well enough to touch him, and remove it. "Please."

"We're all maxed out on employees. Can't hire anyone new. But even if I could, you know I can't go against your mama. Did you try Lombardo's?"

"I've tried everywhere."

"I'm sorry, Dominique."

"It's okay," I say. "Thanks anyway."

* *

I'm alone in the back room, prepping jackets to go out to the dry cleaner and feeling pretty freaking hopeless.

There are only two options. I could explain to Ben that I'm too broke to visit him, and maybe he could get me the money somehow. But even after telling him where we live and that we're not exactly rich, he still doesn't understand what that means. He can't. And honestly? I don't know if I really want him to understand.

And there's the other option. The option I don't even want to think about: not to go. To tell him I'm sorry, but it's too late and he missed his chance and he shouldn't have waited so long to text me. Mono or no mono, he should have tried.

I put a black trench coat on a hanger and hook it on the dry-cleaning rack. As I'm smoothing out the wrinkles, I notice a bulge in one of the pockets. People leave all sorts of stuff in their pockets, then blame us if it gets damaged in the wash. Like the exploding-pen incident when I was in fifth grade. A woman screamed at my mom for half an hour because she'd forgotten to take a pen out of her own pants. When she ran them through our washers, ink got all over the rest of her clothes. After she was finished yelling, Mom quietly handed her the money back, then spent the next two hours scrubbing pen marks out of the machine with rubbing alcohol.

I reach my hand in the coat pocket. It's not a pen or a pair of gloves. It's money. Like, a lot of money.

I count it. It's all twenties. Fourteen twenties, to be exact — $280.

I look at the tag Mom has scribbled on in red ink and attached to the jacket: "L. Petersen."

I don't recognize that name.

I don't think she's a regular.

If L. Petersen can just take out $280 and slip it into her coat pocket and forget it like it's nothing, she can obviously afford to lose it.

I need it more than she does.

It's fate, I convince myself.

It's a sign Ben and I are meant to be together.

Here's the worst part: it doesn't even occur to me to do the right thing.

I shove it into my backpack and pretend it never happened.

* *

I stuff things into my shopping basket like I'm one of those spoiled rich girls on TV. Well, I'm at the Salvation Army on Sixth Street and not Urban Outfitters, but still. A long, flowy silk halter dress that ties with a velvet cord around the neck. A small, woven cross-body purse with two tiny pom-poms on the zipper. A stick of expensive eyeliner with the plastic still on it. A pair of black satin ballet flats — worn but exactly my size. I know I'm not going to have this kind of money again for a long time, maybe forever, so I should save some of it. But I can't help it. I keep shoving more and more things in the plastic basket. A silver necklace with an iridescent stone that looks like an opal. Metallic nail polish. Nothing even remotely practical. As I stand in the fitting room with the dress and the purse and the shoes, I look in the mirror and see myself transforming into the person I've always wanted to be. The person Ben would be proud to be seen with. For the first time in ten days I smile.

{ 4 2 }

Ben

Mom and Dad pretend not to notice the black scuffed indentation on the living room wall, but it's pretty hard to miss. That night, Milo and my dad are watching *Friends* reruns on TV, but I can tell Milo's gaze is shifted slightly to the right. He's staring at the mark. I want to yell that it's no big deal and to stop focusing on it, but if I did that, I'd probably look even more crazy than I already am.

Is Milo right? *Am* I crazy? Just because I'm not what he thinks a brother should be, he's accusing me of ...

Beethoven moved thirty-nine times because he forgot to pay his rent. His house was filled with rotting food — I bet he forgot to eat, too. He'd bang on the piano all night long and his neighbors couldn't stand him. He'd fly into explosive rages, sometimes for no reason at all. He was temperamental and volatile and no one understood him, but he channeled everything, every ounce of passion he had, into his music. What would have happened if someone had forced him to go on medication or see a therapist? Would he have been as brilliant? Maybe he would have stopped composing altogether. Just because he wasn't the textbook definition of "normal," the world would never have had his nine symphonies, nine concertos and hundreds of other works. Operas and sonatas and string quintets and piano trios and bagatelles and …

No. I can't let anyone take my fire away from me. I just need to learn how to master it. I need to sleep more. I need to eat more. And besides, I'm feeling much better now. I have the situation under control. I'm fine.

* *

The next night, when I'm supposed to be sleeping (but I'm sitting on the floor of my bedroom in the dark, restringing again from scratch), I hear my parents whispering. I can only catch snippets of their conversation, so it sounds like "whisper-whisper-whisper-at least he's playing again," "whisper-whisper-whisper-he's out of bed and that's all that matters," "whisper-whisper-whisper-back to school on Monday," "whisper-whisper-whisper-extra sessions with Yaz."

When they talk to me, they're all happy and "isn't it a beautiful day" and "let's open the window and get some of this fresh air in here," even though it's cloudy and windy and 58 degrees. Mom says she knows for a fact it's mono, and we don't have to go to the doctor because she's a nurse and she's seen a million cases. It's not like there's any treatment. I look up the symptoms online, and it does sound a lot like what I had or maybe still have: headache, extreme fatigue, body aches. It all makes sense on paper. But you can only get mono once. This has happened to me before.

It happened last winter. Isaac Nadelstein was guest-conducting the Brahms Violin Concerto in D Major and I wanted to be the soloist more than anything. As a first-year my chances were awful, but I knew if I could just prove to everyone that I was the best, they'd have no choice but to give it to me. In high school I'd always had to balance violin with math and English and all my other subjects, but Brighton was the first time I could put every ounce of my energy into playing. Brahms's concerto was all I could think about. At night when I couldn't sleep I'd write these lists of questions to ask Nadelstein about the piece. Sometimes they were thirty pages long. At first I'd just wait outside Lincoln Center until I saw him, but then one day I couldn't help myself and followed him home.

Even while I was doing it, I knew I shouldn't be. But he's been my idol since I was eight years old, and I figured just knowing where he lived couldn't hurt. He's in this amazing high-rise on the Upper West Side, all steel and picture windows. I watched him go into the lobby, and a few minutes later a light on the sixth floor flicked on. So I zeroed in on his apartment and tried to absorb some of his talent through osmosis. I even got it into my head that maybe if he noticed me standing out there, he'd come down and invite me in and we could spend the night eating Thai takeout and talking about the Brahms. I told myself I was going to stand outside for only ten or fifteen minutes — but the reports from the school said it was four hours.

So they forced me to take two months off to rest and talk to some judgy psychologist at New York Medical Center about my "progress." She told my parents she thought the pressure of being a new student at Brighton had triggered some anxiety. As long as I managed my stress, she deemed me okay to go back to school again. And for a while, I was.

But here's the part I'd never tell anyone. Even now I still think the whole Nadelstein thing was worth it. Even if it didn't turn out exactly as I planned, I made a name for myself at school. I went from being another faceless first-year to Ben, the brilliant, temperamental kid who almost got the solo. I thought I understood how to keep things from getting so out of control this time, but I made a mistake somewhere. I just have to be more careful. I haven't even tried to play *Kreutzer* again yet. I'm taking it easy, sticking with slow scales. They sound simple, but they're the best way to listen for raw tone quality, since there's nothing to hide behind. It's just me and the violin. But everything about it still sounds wrong.

At our sessions Yaz tells me he can detect a slight wavering in my tone, which he's never heard before. He says it happens even to the best players. That I'm overthinking. That if I just take deep breaths, maybe start meditating, eventually it will work itself out. I know he's wrong, though. It has to be the strings.

Mom wants me to stay home and rest on Friday, but my legs are live wires and my arms are lightning bolts, so when she leaves for work I wait fifteen minutes, then throw on a wrinkled undershirt and run to Lincoln Center. I try to slow down, to wait for the light to change before I go tearing across the street, but I can't. It's like once my legs start moving they won't stop. There's only one speed — prestissimo, prestissimo, prestissimo. They don't stop when I push through Brighton's double doors and run across the lobby and past the auditorium and the rows of classrooms and all the way to the back of the building, where there's a line of glass-enclosed practice rooms. They don't stop until I hear the first movement of *Kreutzer* coming from practice room six.

I don't even have to look to know it's them. I duck down behind the door and press my ear to the wood. I don't care who sees me. I have to hear what's so fucking fantastic about Carter. What he can do that I can't. Why he's replacing me. Why he's stealing my piece, my friends, my life.

The first phrase. The land mine. He comes in like a cloud. Effortless, yet remarkably precise. Claire's notes sound calm with him. He's not guiding her. She's soaring on her own. Something she'd never have been able to do if she were playing with me, the scene stealer, the one who makes everything too complicated.

By the time they reach the end of the first movement, I understand. The door opens and my shoulder smashes into something hard and cold. I'm on the floor. Carter is staring down at me, with his violin still tucked under his chin.

"Hi," he says.

"Hi," I say.

"We don't have to tell Yaz about this."

"Tell Yaz. I don't care anymore."

"We're worried about you, Ben."

I turn my head and see Claire on the piano bench in the corner. She doesn't look worried at all. She looks like she wants me to leave.

I jump up and fix my shirt, trying to be casual and normal, even though I'm sweating and my hip burns. "You sounded off on the first phrase, Carter. Might want to focus a little more right up top. You're wavering. And at Claire's entrance —"

He sees right through me.

"Okay, man, thanks."

I feel Carter's fingerprints burning into my arms. His hand on my back, on my shoulder.

"Stop touching me."

"Can we help you get somewhere? Your next class? Robertson's office?"

"Just stop touching me. Don't you want to know where I've been?"

I'm the only one in the room moving. I'm the only one making a sound.

"No?" I ask. "No one gives a shit? Well, I've had mono, if you care. Horribly contagious. Wouldn't want you to catch it."

"I'm sorry, Ben," Claire says.

But I can tell she's thinking about last winter.

"You're not sorry. Neither of you are. I'll let you get back to your masterpiece." I shut the door and run back down the hall and past the classrooms and out the double doors and past the fountain and all the way home.

The hours I've spent tearing open phrases and reconstructing them in my brain. The days I've spent pouring over each note with Yaz. The hours — years — I've spent awake. The friends I never had time to make. Everything I've given up. It all melts away.

As I run, the sidewalk rumbles. The stoplights snap off. The buses tip over. Every skyscraper in Manhattan collapses. First the Empire State Building, then the Chrysler Building, then the Freedom Tower. As I stumble through the mess and the rubble and the dust, I smile. In Dominique's eyes, I'm still normal.

Third Movement
Presto

{ 4 3 }

Dominique

My silk dress swishes against my ankles as I walk, tickling my skin. I glance down at my feet, which look dainty and bohemian and actually kind of beautiful. You know, for feet. I see my reflection in the window of a boutique, and for the first time I look exactly like a girl who should be walking up Park Avenue to meet her boyfriend. I belong. I try to push down the guilty feeling creeping up my stomach and into my chest.

I turn right on Twentieth Street. At the next block I see Ben, leaning against a black gate. Just past him is an explosion of color, a garden full of trees with changing fall leaves and bright yellow bushes and impeccably manicured, brilliant green grass. His hair hangs in his face, and he's staring at the sidewalk. I wonder what he's thinking about.

"Hi," I say, tapping him on the shoulder.

"You're here," he says.

He seems relieved. And then he's hugging me, gripping me hard, pulling me in for a kiss. I can taste his toothpaste and feel the scruff on his chin. It's the first time I've ever seen him with stubble. It makes him look older and somehow cuter — if that's even possible.

"I'm sorry," I say, the words muffled in his jacket. He tells me it's okay, and that I could have told him the truth from the beginning. And that he's sorry he didn't respond sooner. He was so sick he didn't even check his e-mail. I'm relieved, but deep down I'm also surprised. Why is he so quick to forgive me? I mean, I made up another identity and lied to him for weeks. I'm not sure *I'd* forgive me. But I'm so relieved and I need this moment so much I don't want to do anything to jeopardize it.

He hugs me harder, like he's trying to hold on to me. I can feel his breathing, jagged and uneven, and for a second I wonder if something else is wrong. Then he lets go and smiles wide, and I'm too stunned to speak. I push away a piece of hair that's caught in his eyelashes. He takes a step back and opens his arms in a flourish, reciting a speech I can tell he's practiced.

"A Train, I'd like to welcome you to your One Perfect Day. We're starting with the world's most perfect weather, which I really had nothing to do with, but that just means the universe is working in tandem with us today. Are you ready to begin phase one?"

"Phase one? That sounds like we're on a construction site."

At first I think he's angry, but then he twists his lips into an amused smirk. "Okay, what should we call it?"

"Chapter one."

"Are you ready for your first chapter, A Train?"

"Never been more ready in my life."

He holds out a fist, then opens his hand to reveal a small silver key.

"The mayor finally gave you the key to the city?"

"Better. My friend Amy lent me her family's key to Gramercy Park. Only a couple hundred people in the whole entire city have one of these. Jacob Astor had one. John Steinbeck had one. Julia Roberts has one. And now — for the morning, at least — you and I have one."

I shield my eyes from the sun as he clicks the key in the lock. The gate opens, and a carpet of colored leaves sprawls before us. It might be the most beautiful thing I've ever seen. I can tell Ben feels the same way, because he's completely still and silent next to me. We have the entire city block, draped in yellow and red and green and orange and pink, all to ourselves.

At first we can't decide where to sit. We try one empty bench, then think the view might be better from the bench across the tiny paved sidewalk. No, maybe it would be better over by that tall maple tree. Or next to that shrub that looks like a flowering birthday cake.

In the sun it's warm enough to take off our coats. He drapes his arm around my shoulder and it fits, like it was always meant to be there. Like I was born with his arm wrapped around me, and I've had to search my whole life just to get back to it.

"Do you think this is Julia Roberts's usual spot?" I ask.

"Nah, I think she sits over by the gate so people walking by can see her. I bet this is where John Steinbeck would hide away with his notebook and write about loneliness." He kisses my head. "Glad it's not the lonely bench anymore."

The longer we sit, watching the falling leaves, the more I can see myself fitting here. The real me — my flaws, my past, everything I'm embarrassed about, everything, everything, everything. And I want Ben at the center of it all, making me feel safe and loved and protected.

After what seems like hours of saying nothing at all, he asks, "So are you ready for phase two?"

"Time to lay the cement?"

"Yep, put on your hard hat and let's go."

He kisses me, sweet and messy and wonderful. Then he jumps up and races through the garden — I have to run to keep up with him. Billows of flowered silk trail behind me.

* *

He lifts his arm to hail a cab, and one pulls right up. Even though I've come to the city so many times in the last few weeks, riding in a cab is the one thing I've still never done. It's somehow glamorous and terrifying at the same time — it's exactly like you see in movies, except the driver is going about fifteen times faster and doesn't have any regard for pedestrians, bikers, other drivers or general traffic laws. Ben rests his hand on my leg the whole time.

We pull up to a tiny storefront with a sign that reads Hermanita Ecuadorian Kitchen.

Before I can say anything, Ben grabs my hand and tells me, "One day I'll really take you to Ecuador, but we'll have to save that for One Perfect Week."

I throw my arms around him and don't let go until a gigantic feast is laid out in front of us: *fritada* (this really crispy fried pork), *humita* (kind of like corn tamales) and *carne en palito* (grilled steak with plantains), and mashed *yucca* (like sweet and starchy mashed potatoes) and yellow rice and lentils. I even get brave and try a few spoonfuls of tripe, and it isn't as bad as I expected. Ben tells the waiter I'm half Ecuadorian, so he calls me "*hermanita,*" which means "little sister," for the rest of our lunch.

The thing is, though, we keep ordering dish after dish, but Ben isn't eating much. Maybe a bite here and a bite there, but not enough to justify the amount of food he's ordering. At first I'm dizzy with the excess, with all the choices. But then I try to remember the last time my mom and I even ate in a restaurant together. I feel terrible that this food will go to waste when we leave. I wonder what Ben would think if I had it all wrapped up and carried it around for the rest of the day. At the last minute I decide not to, but seeing all the barely touched plates of food being carried back to the kitchen makes me feel sick.

He orders *morocho*, white corn pudding (ugh, more food) for dessert, and now I can feel nervous sweat pricking the back of my neck. This is too much, too big, too fast. But then, as we're waiting for the pudding to come, Ben takes my hands in his, and time stops. I'm drunk from staring into his eyes, and I realize this is the first time we've ever eaten a meal together. He clears his throat and I can tell he's getting ready to recite another speech.

"Dom," he begins, eyes dancing, energy pulsing through his fingertips. "I can't make you do anything you don't want to do. But at this exact second we're less than a mile away from your dad."

So that's what this has been about. I cover my face with my hands and try to control myself.

"I know you're scared," he says. "And you don't want to have a relationship with him, especially if he's a bad guy. But please. It doesn't have to be today. I just know it will make you feel better if you're honest with him. Like you were honest with me. You don't have to say anything. You could just go to his house, spit in his face and leave. Or stomp on his foot. Or just ask him about his life. Or ask him to help you with some money for college. But show him something real, Dom. Show him how much he missed by not being there. Turn this obstacle into the best thing that's ever happened to you."

I cover my face with a napkin and try not to totally embarrass myself by bawling in this little restaurant. But I know Ben's right. In that moment his advice is the greatest thing anyone could ever give me.

Permission to speak up.

Permission to be brave.

Permission to be unstoppable.

{44}

Ben

Chapter three of One Perfect Day: I take Dominique to see a dance recital at Alvin Ailey, her favorite company. The seats are right in the front, and we're so close we can see the sweat and spit spraying off the dancers. This is nothing like the stuffy ballets my mom used to drag Milo and me to when we were kids. Instead of tutus, the dancers are wearing minimal black shorts, and tube tops that blend in with their skin. Their impossibly muscular bodies contort into even more impossible shapes. I can't believe these people are even real their bodies are so ripped. Like living sculptures. I think of Dom wearing one of these outfits and I get totally distracted and then I look down at my shirt and I realize I'm sweating almost as much as the dancers are. I excuse myself to go to the bathroom, and it feels like it's seven million miles away, and I'm running, and I fling open the door and splash water on my face, but it doesn't do much. I stare at myself in the mirror. You have to get it together. Please. You have to.

* *

Chapter four: I take Dominique out dancing at the Copacabana.

It sounded great in my head. For some reason, when I original-ly thought of the idea, I pictured us both as excellent salsa dancers, like those people you see on TV with glittering gowns and suit jackets covered in sequins and wingtip shoes and gelled-back hair. But in reality we're on the dance floor with all these couples who can actually do the steps, like really do them, and I realize that I forgot one tiny thing: I'm the worst thing that's ever happened to dancing. The absolute worst.

At first I keep stepping on her toes, and she's wearing these little flats, so every time I step on them, I accidentally knock her shoe off. Then I actually step right on her toenail and she yelps a little, but I think she tries to pretend it doesn't hurt.

My mind is still flying, and sixteenth notes are cartwheeling on the ceiling, but Dominique helps me keep my focus off them. I wish I hadn't eaten so many plantains, and my heart is thrashing around so hard I think my rib cage is going to turn to dust, but she doesn't notice any of that. She only sees the guy who can solve all her problems. The person who can sweep her off her feet, help her confront her dad and fix everything that's wrong in her life in one single, perfect day. Today I'm a hero.

Then she says something. She's noticed.

"Hey, you're moving really fast. Like, twice as fast as the music. Everything okay?"

"Sorry. I'm a terrible dancer."

"And you're breathing really fast. Do you want to take a break?"

"No, no, no, I want to keep going." I grab her around the waist and try to dip her. She almost topples backward and has to grab my shoul-ders to get her balance.

"Hang on, let's just take it slower. I know some of the steps. Follow me."

She puts my right hand on her left shoulder and holds my left hand in her right. She stands with her feet together, then steps forward with her left foot, rocks back with her right foot and steps back on her left again. I try to mimic her, imagining each step is a note, and then she's pushing against my hand with her shoulder, guiding us in a circle as we dance. I raise my arm and she does a twirl underneath it. But she doesn't just do a regular, 360-degree turn. She spins, like, three times in a row. I didn't even know you could do that.

She's an incredible dancer. When you watch her, everything clicks. I've never seen someone make a wrist flick look sexy and fluid and passionate all at once, but somehow she does. Together we're like one of those standardized test analogies: She is to dance as I am to music. It's suddenly, indisputably clear that this is what she needs to be doing with her life. And somehow, with her on my arm, I'm incredible, too.

"How'd you learn to do this?" I ask.

"I took dance for ten years. That part was true."

"Dom. You're really good. It's like your legs are made of … magic. Or rainbows. Or glittery Jell-O. Or —"

"Hey, Ben?"

"Yeah?"

"You're stepping on my foot again."

* *

The last chapter of One Perfect Day is the trickiest to coordinate. I've been waiting for this all day. Years. Lifetimes.

We have one more hour before we have to be back downtown for my last surprise. It's a beautiful night, so we grab slices of pizza and walk toward Central Park.

"Where are we going?" Dominique holds on to my arm, just like I've seen a million other couples do in movies.

"To the golden age," I say.

I stick my hand in my pocket and feel for the two tickets to the midnight screening of *Singin' in the Rain* that I bought online. Just to make sure.

As we walk, I can feel my breath slowing and the visions fading away. Everything's going to be okay. I've got this. Dominique makes this broken, hopeless semblance of a life feel whole and complete again. All I have to do is put my hand in hers and keep walking, and I know everything will work out. It has to.

"Wait," she says, stopping short and tugging on my arm. "This is where we first met. Right here, on this sidewalk square."

We're standing outside Carnegie Hall. I look down at the sidewalk. It's glittering, but I can't tell if there are little slivers of mica embedded in the cement, or it's just another thing my mind is making up.

"I thought we met at the fountain."

"No. When I was on the field trip. I was standing in line for my bus, and you walked by me and gave me the world's sexiest look, at this very spot."

I pull her in close so we're both standing in the square together. I lean in and wrap my arms around her.

"Right here?"

Right here, I met the only person in the world who can save me from this mess.

{ 45 }

Dominique

I glance up at the sky. There's one faint white light cutting through the blackness.

"Look, there's a star," I say. I'm wrapped in him. An extra layer of Ben. A layer that, now that I've felt it, I don't know how I'm ever going to live without. I whisper a silent prayer to the star: Thank you, thank you, thank you for letting him understand. Thank you for letting me keep him.

He hugs me harder now, and we stay that way for a few minutes, twisted into each other, gazing up at the sky. I hold him as tight as I can to block the wind.

"Hey," I say, breaking the silence at last. "Do you think someone lives up there?" I point up to the top floor of Carnegie Hall, at the curtained window Cass and I spotted. The lights are off inside, so the window just looks like a dark rectangle now.

"There used to be. There were a bunch of apartments on the top few floors. Andrew Carnegie built them to house artists — at that time the concert hall wasn't doing too great and he needed the extra rent money."

"Wait, you're telling me that at some point Andrew Carnegie was broke?" I imagine him sitting on the floor of the stage, eating rice and beans and beans and beans every night to save money.

"Completely ridiculous, right? That's obviously not an issue for the Carnegie estate anymore, so a few years ago they decided to evict everyone and turn the apartments into rehearsal rooms. This one lady, Editta Sherman — she lived right there. They nicknamed her the 'Duchess of Carnegie Hall.' She was a photographer, and she lived in this massive rent-controlled apartment for, like, sixty years. It made the news because they evicted her, but she refused to leave. Even after everyone else in the building was gone. I remember looking up when I came here for concerts with my parents and seeing the light on in her window. When she was almost a hundred, she finally agreed to move. I always wondered what happened to her. And then, a few years ago, there was an obituary."

"Hers?"

"Yeah. Would it have been so terrible to just let her stay here? She was a hundred years old and they ripped her out of her home. They really needed one more music rehearsal room that badly? Another place for a bunch of stupid violin players to play things dead people wrote?"

The doors under the brightly lit awning open and people pour out onto the street, all dressed up in suit jackets and gold watches and small red, boxy purses and high heels that look like torture devices. A concert must have ended.

"Let's go," Ben says abruptly, grabbing my hand.

We push past the crowd, like tiny fish swimming against the current. There's so much chaos in the lobby, with people rushing to leave and putting on their coats and shuffling through their programs, that the ushers don't notice Ben leading me through an unmarked side door and down a long corridor.

I follow him along an endless hallway, past a lot of doors with what look like offices inside. I'm struck by how nice it all is. No one sees this part of the building, and yet it's almost as beautiful as the stage itself. Framed music posters from all sorts of concerts line the walls. I don't recognize any of them, but I assume they must be famous musicians who played at Carnegie Hall. We turn left, then right, then left, then left again. I wonder how many times Ben has been back here. By the way he's acting he's done this a million times.

"Are you sure you know where you're going?" I ask.

"Not really, but we'll figure it out." He looks back at me with wild eyes. Why are they so bloodshot?

"Wait, what if we get in trouble?" I whisper.

"Don't be ridiculous, A Train. Things like that don't happen on One Perfect Day."

He has a harsh edge to his voice that I've never heard before. But what scares me most are his eyes. It's like he's looking through me. Like I'm not even here.

"We're definitely not supposed to be back here," I say, louder this time.

"Then they shouldn't have left the door unlocked."

We climb an iron spiral staircase for what feels like forever. Twisting up and up and up and up. Ben keeps going faster until he's at least a floor above me, but I can hear his footsteps. I keep thinking some guard with handcuffs is going to pop out any second. God, this is stupid. Why am I doing this? Like I'm not in enough trouble as it is.

My heart thrashes in my chest. Turn around, turn around, turn around, it pleads. I keep climbing. Something's not right.

I go up and up until I see Ben again. He's standing in another long hallway with a row of doors. Outside each door is a small engraved plaque: ARCHIVES RESEARCH ROOM. ORCHESTRA ROOM. GREEN ROOM. PRACTICE ROOM A. PRACTICE ROOM B. PRACTICE ROOM C.

THE STUDIO ROOM.

"I think this is it," he says. Eyes glassy, hair wet and messy.

He tries the door. It's locked.

"It's okay," I say. "It's cool getting to see what it's like up here. Let's go back down."

But he doesn't hear me. He's rummaging through his pockets, spilling receipts on the floor. He drops his phone and I pick it up, but he doesn't even say thank you.

"Hey, you okay?" I ask.

Nothing.

Tissues rain to the ground. I had no idea one person could cram so much junk into a single pair of dress pants.

"Ben," I say, even louder.

"What?"

"Let's go back."

"Wait."

"This is making me too nervous. Let's go. Please, let's go."

"Just a second."

He opens his wallet and takes out his MetroCard. He carefully slides it up and down in the space between the door and the wall. He jiggles the doorknob, trying to pop the Studio Room's lock.

There must be security guys in this building. One of them is going to walk down this hallway any second. Every creak, every shadow, makes me jump.

"I really don't think we should be doing this," I say. "They know how to install decent locks at Carnegie Hall. I don't think it's, like, a bedroom-door lock that you can just jam open with a credit card."

"Got it," Ben says, and the door swings wide.

This whole thing makes me want to throw up. What if the security guard calls the cops when he finds us, and we end up in jail overnight? Ben would get out immediately, of course, but my mom could never afford to bail me out. I'd have to sit in jail forever with a bunch of murderers.

Ben grabs my hand, pulls me in, shuts the door and locks it behind us. My nervousness fades a little when I see how beautiful the view is. Floor-to-ceiling windows line two of the walls. Midtown is bathed in sparkling light. The ceilings are so high just looking at them makes the room spin. There's no furniture except for the stack of chairs and music stands lined up in the corner. Otherwise it's sparse and grand and clean, with blond hardwood floors and creamy white walls. And there, on a long track that extends across the length of the windows, are the red drapes, pulled back in the corner.

"So this is where the Duchess lived?" I ask.

"Yep, this is the place."

"Wow. I can't believe one woman lived in here all by herself. It's huge. It's unbelievable." Way too big for me and Cass. Or me and Ben.

"Do you think we should move in?" he asks, putting his arms around me.

I melt into him and forget everything. I fall. I forget there could be cameras and I forget how nervous I am and I forget the uneasy feeling in my stomach. I dive, headfirst, back into our dream.

"Well, we'd put the couch over here," I say, pointing by the window. "I've always wanted a big white overstuffed couch with lots of throw pillows. And a cozy blanket draped across the arm, for when it gets cold."

He twirls me on the shining hardwood. "What goes over here?" he asks, pointing to a corner by the door.

"A big bookcase, like the one at your house but taller, and bigger, and full of first editions."

"Done, done, done!" Ben says, running around the perimeter of the big, empty room. "This is all ours, and we'll fill it with everything you've ever wanted. What about a sculpture collection here? And we'll have to have music. We'll need an old phonograph. And these window treatments are no good at all. No, no, we'll need something bigger, grander, on every window, cascading to the floor. And we'll have to install a kitchen with granite countertops. And a washer and dryer. And the master bath with a Jacuzzi tub can go right in this corner, out of the way, just next to the master bedroom."

I stand back by the door, and he keeps going, like a windup toy. Running around and around the room in circles. It takes me a minute to realize: I don't think he can stop. I try to get a word in, but he's not listening.

"Wait, Ben? Do you hear me?"

"And a collection of priceless instruments, right on this wall. Coltrane's sax and Armstrong's trumpet and Nadelstein's violin. Hey, I wonder what the view is like from up here." He shoves open one of the massive windows and jumps up on the ledge.

My skin surges with cold sweat.

"Ben, get down. You're really freaking me out, okay?"

"God, it's beautiful. You can see every star in the world from up here. Come over."

"Please, please get down!"

"Dominique, you have to see this."

He kneels, presses his stomach against the sill and edges his way outside, then stands back up again, so that his back is pressing against the windowpane. Outside. My legs are frozen — if I walk over to the window, I'm afraid I'll distract him and he'll slip. But if I stand here, I'm afraid he'll go out farther and do something even more dangerous. Is he trying to climb up on the roof? His feet are trembling. He's going to lose his footing. I know it. He's going to lose his balance and fall.

There's only one thing I can think of to do. I quickly flip the lock, fling the door open and yell down into the stairwell. "Help me!" I scream, as loud as I can. My voice echoes back down to the lobby. "Help! Is anyone here? Please!"

A man's voice cuts through the silence. "Hello? Is someone up there? Hello?"

That's when it ends.

{ 46 }

Ben

Page 7 of 83

Interview #3: Milo Tristan

Relationship to patient: Younger brother

Q: What do you recall about that day, Milo?

MT: I remember waking up early and sitting in bed for a few minutes. I'd gone out with my girlfriend the night before and was pretty tired. Then I got up and was on my way to the bathroom to brush my teeth, and I remember walking through the hallway and seeing Ben getting dressed in his room.

Q: The door was open?

MT: Yeah. He was, uh … um, he was shaking and talking to himself and getting dressed in this really nice suit that he only usually wears for recitals, which was weird because it was, like, 7:30 in the morning. He's a violinist. You already know that. But anyway. I knew my parents wouldn't want him leaving the apartment, because he'd been really sick that week. But I thought if I could just be home with my parents alone, I could finally convince them that he needed help.

Q: What time did he leave?

MT: I think he ended up leaving around eight.

Q: And your parents were both home at this point?

MT: No, my mom was grocery shopping and my dad was still asleep. So now I'm just waiting for her to come home, and I'm nervous because I keep thinking Ben's going to come back before she does, or she's going to decide to run more errands. But she came back around ten and I asked her to go into Ben's room with me.

Q: And you showed her what was in the closet.

MT: Yeah. And I was also nervous because my parents never really wanted to listen when I'd tell them I thought something was wrong with Ben. It's almost like they let him do anything because he's this musical genius and they don't want to mess with his talent or his process. My mom was in complete denial at that point, but if she saw this, I knew she'd finally understand. She had to.

Q: Would you mind telling me about it?

MT: [Sighs] Okay. I've been trying to figure out how to describe it. Like, nothing I could say could do it justice. It was like a spider web made of steel. There must have been ten thousand violin strings stretching from one side of the closet to the other, winding together in patterns. It looked infinite. Like it took him thousands — maybe millions — of hours to complete. They were looped around pushpins and tacked to the wall, to the ceiling, to the floor, everywhere. There were so many strings it was almost like metallic fabric. You could barely even see the walls behind it. And then I looked more closely and noticed, uh, the floor was covered with wood — shards and splinters and chunks. Like wood chips. I knew his old violin was missing from the living room, but I thought he'd just taken it into his bedroom to play it or something. But he'd destroyed it. We waited hours for him to get home. My mom was crying. Then she was furious. My dad just kept pacing back and forth through the living room, shaking his head. We called Yaz and Claire and some of his friends at school. No one had seen him. His friends — Jun-Yi and Jacob and Kelly — actually said they'd been avoiding him the last few months because he was acting so weird. I'd wondered why I hadn't seen any of them in a while. So we finally pulled up the online statement for his credit card. The one my dad gave him for emergencies. I have one, too, and I've maybe used it once. But there were thousands of dollars in charges from the last week. Seventeen pages of different kinds of strings, at $130 each. Dozens of violin bows, every one of them costing more than a year of his college tuition, Mom told me. Two tickets for $200 each to La Bohème. A room at the Four Seasons for $1,700. We called to see if he was there, but he hadn't checked in yet. Finally he walked in around midnight, and at this point I didn't even want to look at him. But it was hard not to. His eyes were wild, just darting all over the room like he'd done drugs or something. I know my brother and I know he'd never do that, but something was seriously wrong.

Q: Did he say where he had been all day?

MT: He said he was with his girlfriend, and they'd snuck into Carnegie Hall and the guard kicked them out. Threatened to call the cops but didn't. It's weird, because none of us ever met her. His girlfriend. I asked a few of his friends at school and they'd never seen her, either. And since then, since he's been in the hospital, he hasn't said anything about her at all.

Q: What are you thinking, Milo?

MT: I don't want to accuse him of it. She seemed real. The way he talked about her. But now I don't know.

{47}

Dominique

I have to imagine I'm holding Ben's hand as I walk down the street. It's the only way I can work up enough courage to do this.

I look up at the street signs on the corner. Second Avenue and 121st Street. Spanish Harlem. I've never even seen his building before, but I have the apartment number memorized from the return address on his once-a-year birthday cards: 178 121st St., #6G. New York, NY 10035.

And there it is, a red brick building with six floors. Just some pavement and a few bricks separating me from him. The ground floor is a bodega. Behind one of the dirty windows above it is my father's apartment. His bed. His toothbrush. His couch. I'm not sure if he lives alone or with roommates or with some other woman or what. But I have to find out.

I pretend Ben is gripping my hand as I walk up to the front stoop and ring the buzzer. I don't breathe.

A man with a big blue duffel bag pushes the front door open and walks past me down the steps. I catch the door with my foot and go inside.

There's no elevator, so I walk up the six flights to get to the top floor. It reminds me a lot of my building — overflowing trash bags in the corner of the lobby, a loose banister that's probably more dangerous if you hold it than if you don't. Sticky linoleum steps, crumbly at the corners.

When I get to the top of the stairs, I'm covered in a layer of icy sweat. I grab Ben's hand as tight as I can and ring the doorbell.

A little girl opens the door. I'm pretty bad at guessing kids' ages, but she's probably somewhere between four and six. Her hair is in a long braid with a little plastic bead tied to the end. She's holding a pancake with a bite taken out of it and her hands are coated with syrup.

"Hi. Is, um, Reg home?" Freaking Reg.

"Who?"

"Reg?" I squeak out.

The little girl scrunches up her nose.

At first I can't say it. It's like trying to gargle rocks. "Um, your dad," I manage at last. "Is your dad home?"

"Ohhh. Yeah!"

So he has a daughter. A daughter who isn't me.

"*Papá, ven aquí.*" She speaks Spanish. Of course she does.

A woman in a tank top and yoga pants runs in from a back room and shoos her daughter away from the door. Her thick, long hair is in a ponytail and her skin is darker than mine. She's beautiful. She looks younger than my dad. I wonder where he met her. I wonder if she's as kind and good-hearted and hardworking as my mom, or if she's just some second-rate replacement.

"Sorry," the woman tells me. "She knows she's not supposed to answer the door. Can I help you?"

"Hi," I say. "Um, is Reg here?"

She raises her eyebrows. "I'm his wife. Can I help you with something?"

In the other room I hear silverware and glasses clinking. I try to remember the last time my mom and I actually sat down to eat breakfast together. And never pancakes. Something healthy and practical. Not frivolous and indulgent, like pancakes. I feel hot, tingling jealousy wash over me.

"No, you can't help me," I say.

"Excuse me?"

"I said, 'No, you can't help me.' I'm sorry. There's something I need to ask him."

"If you're selling something —"

"I'm his daughter," I blurt out.

Her face softens. "Dominique?"

"Yeah."

"One second." She takes the little girl's hand and they walk back into the room with the clinking silverware.

And then my dad is standing in the doorway in a white T-shirt with a nickel-sized maple syrup stain on his chest. His head is shaved, but his eyelashes are long and dark, just like mine.

"Hi," I say.

"Dominique." I think he's about to say something else, but he doesn't. I always forget how deep and gentle his voice sounds, like a radio announcer's.

"I'm sorry for doing this," I say slowly, trying to keep my voice from breaking. "Interrupting your breakfast with your family. I just —"

Even if I wanted to say something else, I can't, because tears are spilling down my face and I'm hiccuping and gasping and I can't catch my breath. I'm not ready for this. I've always wondered what it would be like to sit on his couch and watch a movie, just me and my dad, hanging out. Now, through the doorway, I can see his couch for the first time: gray with white pillows. But it's covered with some other kid's toys. Even though I could push my way through and sit down on it and turn on the TV, it's never felt farther out of reach.

My dad — Reg, whatever — looks concerned. "What's wrong?"

"I understand why you don't have a relationship with me. Maybe you were too young to be a dad. Maybe I cried all the time when I was a baby and it gave you headaches. I've run through every possible scenario in my head a million times. But whatever the reason was, it doesn't matter. You can't hurt me, because I've never known what having a father is like. You can meet me at Starbucks once every three years and send me a card on my birthday. If that's enough for you, fine, that's enough for me. But how could you do this to Mom? How could you?"

"Honey, your mom and I couldn't get along. You know that. We would have killed each other if —"

"But you left us with nothing. We're stuck in Trenton and we can't get out. And it's terrible. Worse than you could even imagine. Worse than when you were there. Mom's laundromat is barely paying for itself, and I'm never going to be able to make enough money for college, and it's hopeless. How could you just run away and start a new family without even making sure we were going to be okay?"

I deserve better. I realize that now.

"Dominique, you know I don't have any money. If I had it, I'd give it to you."

He hands me a tissue and I dab my face, but it's still covered in tears and snot. "But she has toys. And you're eating pancakes."

"Yes, I try to save enough to provide for Michaela."

"Michaela. Is she your daughter?"

"Yes. Well, she's Maria's, but we've been married for three years now."

Which makes it even worse.

Reg motions for me to come inside, but I shake my head.

He lowers his voice to a whisper. "Dominique, what do you want me to do? You know your mom. It has nothing to do with you. You know you're not the reason I left and you're not why I stayed away. Your mom is ... She's hard to handle. She never wanted me around you. I just wanted to keep the peace. I thought it'd be better for everyone. It's been fifteen years. What could I do to fix things now?"

I grip Ben's hand with all my strength.

"I want to go to college," I say. "And I want you and my mom, together, to figure out how to pay for it. I'll work hard and get better grades and I'll try for scholarships, but I need to know that you'll help me find a way to go."

"But I'm barely —"

"Please. You're my only hope. And I deserve it." Just like anyone else deserves a chance at grace and beauty and art and music. And life.

He wipes his face with his hands. At last he says, "I'll figure something out."

I take one last look inside. On the floor there's a towering stack of kids' movies that's almost as high as the TV. A pink tricycle in the corner. A plastic container of Barbie clothes under the coffee table.

"Sorry for interrupting your breakfast," I mumble.

Then I'm gone. I'm racing down the stairs as fast as I can. Faster and faster, until I push the entryway door open and the cold air hits me.

{48}

Ben

THE BRIGHTON CONSERVATORY
SYMPHONY ORCHESTRA

~ Featuring ~

Carter Strom (1st violin)

Quiao Sung (1st violin)

Wilford Meyer (1st violin)

Sara Lopez (1st violin)

Jon Kerr (1st violin)

Molly Holmes (1st violin)

Erica Kincaid (1st violin)

Alex Howe (1st violin)

Sam Bruce (1st violin)

Brandon Sharp (1st violin)

Lily Benson (1st violin)

Amy Simpson (1st violin)

Muriel Ivey (2nd violin)

Dewei T'an (2nd violin)

Eden Bishop (2nd violin)

Grace Peters (2nd violin)

Alice Monaldo (2nd violin)

Calista Dudek (2nd violin)

Jenn D. Gaines (2nd violin)

Isla Platt (2nd violin)

Mary Dunn (2nd violin)

Eleanor James (2nd violin)

·

Jun-Yi Leng (viola)

Mary Cortez (viola)

Sarah Foley (viola)

James Rodriguez (viola)

Victoria Dias (viola)

Jacob Ozerov Jr. (viola)

Carey Burke (viola)

Luong Phi (viola)

Shawn Baxter (viola)

Suzie Brown (viola)

Akilah Holstetter (viola)

Melissa Roman (viola)

Nahi Khoury (viola)

Malika Conley (viola)

Hadley Dean (viola)

•

Gloria Thames (cello)

Iman Kabourek (cello)

Tony Lucchese (cello)

Marjo Lewis (cello)

Qiao Tien (cello)

David J. Dumond (cello)

Gabriel Silva (cello)

Julia Knutsen (cello)

Jackson Thomas (bass)

Alexis Smith (bass)

Timothy Hinds (bass)

Tom Turner (bass)

Rita Hathaway (bass)

Diane Curran (bass)

Tim Thompson (flute)

Anthony Mack Jr. (flute/piccolo)

•

Ali Smith (oboe/English horn)

Win Han (oboe/English horn)

•

Madison West (clarinet)

Robert Copeland (clarinet)

Jamie Lü (bass clarinet)

•

Eric D'Angelo (bassoon)

Donald Puente (bassoon)

Fabian Williams (contrabassoon)

•

Samiyah Sabbag (horn)

Anne Efremova (horn)

Phil L. Soderstrom (horn)

Fred Werkman (horn)

Leena Chin (trumpet)

Elias Andreasson (trumpet)

•

Jeannie Fisher (trombone)

Kat J. Hassell (trombone)

Sergey Aleks (trombone)

•

Michiyuki Toiguchi (tuba)

Ray Curran (timpani)

Lilli Fleming (percussion)

Frank Dre (percussion)

Kouta Oouchi (percussion)

Gianna Alma (percussion)

Keith L. Jones (percussion)

•

Kelly Pratt (harp)

Park Green (harp)

{49}
Dominique

NEW YORK UNIVERSITY
DEPARTMENT OF DANCE AUDITIONS

Please pick your top three preferred audition times:

Audition candidates are required to learn a ballet combination, a jazz combination and a modern combination. An exam to evaluate rhythmic skills will be conducted to determine placement.

X Sept. 12, 12 p.m.	**X** Sept. 21, 12 p.m.	___ Oct. 3, 12 p.m.
___ Sept. 12, 4 p.m.	**X** Sept. 21, 4 p.m.	___ Oct. 3, 4 p.m.
___ Sept. 13, 2 p.m.	___ Sept. 22, 2 p.m.	___ Oct. 4, 2 p.m.
___ Sept. 13, 4 p.m.	___ Sept. 23, 4 p.m.	___ Oct. 5, 4 p.m.
___ Sept. 14, 7 p.m.	___ Sept. 24, 7 p.m.	___ Oct. 6, 7 p.m.
___ Sept. 15, 8 p.m.	___ Sept. 25, 8 p.m.	___ Oct. 7, 8 p.m.

Following the technical portion of the audition, candidates may be required to perform a solo dance. The piece must be five minutes in length and demonstrate proficiency in at least one of the following styles: modern, ballet, jazz or tap. Please bring sheet music or a flash drive containing an .mp3 of your solo piece. An accompanist will be provided.

Finally, candidates will be interviewed by a New York University Department of Dance faculty member.

Please adhere to the following dress code:

• Leotard and tights for ballet, footless tights for modern dance
• Ballet shoes, jazz shoes and lyrical jazz shoes
• Hair up, off the face and back
• No loose-fitting clothing
• No distracting patterns or colors

{ 5 0 }

Ben

JAYESH MALHOTRA, MD, PhD

NEW YORK PSYCHIATRIC CENTER

Patient Name: Benjamin Tristan

Address: 1480 Lexington Ave., Apt. 1556, New York, NY 10128

LITHIUM CARBONITE capsules, USP, 300 mg

Take one capsule by mouth three times a day.

Quantity: 120; 1 refill remaining

JAYESH MALHOTRA, MD, PhD

NEW YORK PSYCHIATRIC CENTER

Patient Name: Benjamin Tristan

Address: 1480 Lexington Ave., Apt. 1556, New York, NY 10128

BUPROPION HYDROCHLORIDE extended-release tablets, 150 mg

Take one tablet by mouth once a day.

Quantity: 100; 3 refills remaining

JAYESH MALHOTRA, MD, PhD

NEW YORK PSYCHIATRIC CENTER

Patient Name: Benjamin Tristan

Address: 1480 Lexington Ave., Apt. 1556, New York, NY 10128

CLONAZEPAM tablets, 1 mg

Take one tablet nightly before bed.

Quantity: 30; no refills remaining

{ 5 1 }

Dominique

"Paging Miss Fashionably Late. If you don't leave in the next three minutes, you're going to miss your train."

"Okay, okay," I yell to Cass in the living room. Tap shoes, check. Jazz shoes, check. Socks with little rubbery things on the bottoms, check. Change of tights, check. Dance skirt, check. Extra hair ties and bobby pins, check. Lip gloss, check. MetroCard, check.

"Okay," I say, poking my head out of the bedroom. "I'm ready."

Cass gasps in this completely exaggerated way, like he's trying to suck all the air out of the room and into his lungs. "You look gorgeous."

"I'm just wearing dance clothes."

"I don't care. You're going to get it."

"I'm so glad the audition has absolutely nothing to do with my dance aptitude but everything to do with how I look in a pair of tights."

Cass shoos me away, and I run to the kitchen to grab the apple and water bottle my mom left for me on the counter. She's at Spin Cycle, of course. Nothing new there. But she's really excited about this college thing. Now, instead of talking about what we're going to eat for dinner, we talk about what it's going to be like when I move to New York next year. Not that it's a done deal. But there's a scholarship for lower-income students and if we combine that with the money Reg gave me and I take out student loans, it's … possible. Now that there are three of us working together, it's more than just a fantasy. Even just the promise of a plan has made my mom laugh and joke a lot more while she's folding other people's sheets.

And she laughs and shakes her head whenever I say it, but my master plan is to get her to come to the city with me. She could get a job in retail — she folds faster than anyone I know and would probably be the manager by the end of the month — and we could move somewhere more affordable, like Queens or the Bronx, and Cass could move in with us, too. We could all move into one apartment at first, and as everyone starts to make more money expand out and eventually buy the entire building. Mom says I'm nuts when I start talking like this, but for the first time in years I'm actually letting myself dream. Maybe none of it will come true, but there's always a chance.

Mom's been letting me work fewer hours so I can get ready for my audition, and Cass has been coming in to help her on weeknights. His plan is to start community college in the fall and work as many part-time jobs as he can so he can save a bunch of money. When he gets to the city, he wants to work in a restaurant at night and audition for movies during the day. ("Not, like, action movies or anything, though," he says. I tell him he can't be too picky.) I don't think our Carnegie Hall apartment is in the cards, but we'll settle for sharing a studio. We don't need anything fancy. As long as it's ours. Even just month to month.

* *

Taking the train is the simplest thing in the world now, since I started dance classes at a little studio in the East Village. Renee, my old teacher at the community center, told me about some "pay what you can" classes on Saturdays, and I've been going every week, thanks to train money from Reg. My dad.

New Jersey towns speed by the window, like I'm watching a movie in fast-forward. Hamilton, Princeton Junction, New Brunswick, Edison, Metuchen, Metropark, Rahway. They're all places I wished I could live when I was a kid. Now I have a chance to escape them all and live in New York City, the best place in the universe.

Well, if I can nail this audition, get in and get the scholarship. But I can't worry about that now. I just need to give the best audition I possibly can. That's all I can do. Fate will have to do the rest. A boy with black hair walks through the train car, and for a second I think it might be Ben. He's wearing a button-down shirt with a collar like Ben would. But as he passes, his eyes are too light and his nose is all wrong, and I wonder how I even thought it was Ben to begin with.

I hope the real Ben is okay. I hope he's happy.

I see Fake Bens a lot. Someone with his eyes or his hair or his arms will walk past the window of Spin Cycle and I'll get goose bumps. I'll press my palms to the glass, trying not to blink, just in case. But it's never really him. Cass thinks he sees him, too, sometimes. *Ben lookalike on the corner of Washington and Roebling,* he'll text me. *Not as cute as the real one, though.*

Ben sent me a bunch of e-mails right after One Perfect Day. Telling me he was still sick with mono and he couldn't see me because he was contagious. And then that he was away on a family vacation to visit his aunt and uncle in California. And then that school had gotten way too busy and we'd have to meet up in a few more weeks. I knew these things were lies. He'd always end the e-mail with "I'm okay. I hope you're okay, too." But I wasn't. And I knew he wasn't. I just didn't know how to ask what was wrong.

Then, a few months later, he finally told me the truth. He was diagnosed with bipolar disorder, and he had just gotten out of the hospital. He'd been in there for four months. On our One Perfect Day, he was having what his doctors called a "manic episode." He said he barely even remembers it, but was able to put the pieces together with his psychologist. I looked up "manic episode" on Google, and the whole thing really scared me. It could have been so much worse. He's lucky he went to the doctor when he did. And that I yelled for the guard, and he helped me get him down.

And then he apologized. He told me he was sorry for pushing me to sneak into Carnegie Hall when I didn't want to. Sorry for keeping me out too late, even though I needed to go home. And especially sorry for making me feel uncomfortable. (Which was actually a total understatement.)

I wrote back, fingers cramping I was typing so fast, telling him none of those things mattered. I wanted to take him in my arms and wrap him up and make him feel safe, the way he made me feel when I needed it more than anything. I told him to please keep writing to me, even if he didn't want to see me. I didn't tell him — because I didn't want to worry him and make this even harder than it already was — that at the time, his e-mails were the only thing holding me together. Without them, getting up in the morning was pointless. Why even bother to go to school? Why not just melt into a puddle and drip into the gutters on Main Street and get washed away in a rainstorm?

Three excruciating days later he wrote back.

To: hidingbehindcurls@gmail.com
From: lookingforatrain@gmail.com
Subject: You are ...
February 8, 11:12 p.m.
My A Train,

You are the most kind, caring, funny, charismatic, badass, beautiful person I've ever met in my life. I need you to believe me when I say this. When I was sick, I wanted to bottle you up and take you around with me so I could always feel your energy. I thought if I could just figure out a way to do that, I'd be relaxed and happy, like you. But now I'm realizing that's not how it works. I can't save you and you can't save me. We need to stay on our own paths. And right now, I need to know that I can be healthy on my own before I can be healthy with someone else. Please, please understand, A Train. I just need to know I can do this. I know you can, too.

Love, Ben

I e-mailed a couple more times after that. I called him once, leaving a rambling voice mail about wanting to be friends if that's what he wanted and offering to meet by the fountain at Lincoln Center, like we used to. Just to catch up. Just to see how he was doing. But he never called back.

Then it was a week between e-mails.

Then it was two weeks.

And then it was nothing.

No one really ever knew about Ben and me except for Cass. Sometimes I wonder if Ben ever existed in the first place, or if he was just a mirage — appearing when I needed him most, then disappearing back into the crowd as it rushed past Grand Central Station. City anonymity. Hundreds of people moving as one.

There are more than 8.5 million people in New York City. Statistically, I could live here my entire life and never see him again.

I wanted to tell my mom. Especially at the end. But I knew if I tried to describe him from memory, I could never do him justice. The way his eyes got squinty when he smiled. The way his hair fell across his forehead, and just when you thought it was about to fall into his eyes, his fingertips would brush the strands away. The way he'd get excited about something and talk without taking a breath, until he was practically gasping for air. The way he unlocked the whole city, and all its music, and showed me how I fit inside it. The way he gave me the strength to rise out of this mess, and the confidence to dream of something better. Like the life he had. Or I thought he had.

So I just couldn't.

I left him out of the story completely.

One morning at Spin Cycle, Mom came in with a bag of Mrs. Fisher's delicates, like she does every week. I saw her sorting them all carefully into the sink and I knew I had to tell her about seeing my dad. I felt like I was going to throw up, but I started to talk anyway, words flying out of my mouth so fast I wasn't even sure what I'd end up saying.

"Hey, Mom? Can I ask you a question?"

"What, baby?" She pushed her hands into the sudsy water, up to her elbows, like I've seen her do a thousand times.

"Actually, it's not a question. I have something to tell you. Um ... I saw Dad."

"What? Where?"

"In New York."

"What were you doing in New York?"

"I went to see him."

"By yourself?"

"Yeah."

She stopped. "Without asking me."

"Yeah. I'm sorry. I knew you wouldn't want me to."

"How did you get the money to go?"

"I did something really bad."

She pulled her hands out of the water. They were chapped from the cold, all the way up to her forearms, like she was wearing long pink gloves. She wiped her hands on her jeans.

"What? Don't you dare tell me you stole it or you did something illegal or —"

"I found some money in a coat we were sending out for dry cleaning. I'm so sorry. I saved the owner's receipt and I have her contact information, and I almost have enough to pay her back." I was crying then, like a snot-dripping-down-my-face kind of embarrassing cry, and Mom was hugging me and telling me how dumb it was, and I could have just asked for the money, and then I told her that I was afraid of what she'd think, because I knew she hated my dad and didn't want me to have anything to do with him. And then I told her about knocking on the door and the pancakes and his daughter who speaks Spanish, and everything I said to him. And then Mom was telling me how sorry she was that I didn't have a dad in my life, and we were hugging each other and crying so hard that Mom had to lock the store and put the Be Right Back sign in the window.

And then I showed her the note my dad sent in the mail, written on a Wildwood, New Jersey, postcard.

Dominique —

Thank you for coming to visit me. I'm sorry I didn't say that when you were here. I didn't know what to say. I want you to grow up smarter than me. I don't have a lot of money, but I want to help you if I can. I'd like to meet you and your mom for breakfast and talk about college.

— Dad (Reg)

But I never told my mom about Ben, the person who inspired me to do it all in the first place.

Sometimes I wonder if Ben even really loved me to begin with. How could you be preoccupied, obsessed with someone one day, and then the next day just vanish? I know — if he's sick, as sick as he says, he probably isn't in the right mind-set to be in a relationship. He probably doesn't want to hurt me again. But I just wish that this time I could be the one to help him, the way he helped me.

Ben was music. And that's the thing about music, I guess. It begins, it consumes you and then it ends.

* *

I step onto the hot platform at Penn Station and my hair immediately frizzes up. I wore my black tights, hoping they'd show sweat the least, but now I'm wondering if I should have gone with a brighter color, like blue or green, so my legs don't absorb as much heat. I pinch the fabric on my thighs to air them out.

I swipe my MetroCard at the turnstile, push my way through, then double-check the directions I've scribbled down on the audition notice. Take the A, C or E train to West Fourth Street, where I used to tell Ben my dorm was. Walk up to Washington Square Park and look for the tall tan building on the north side with the plaque that says NEW YORK UNIVERSITY. Check in with the security guard, then go up to the twelfth floor.

There's no one else on the platform but me, so I do a few stretches. First position. Second position. Lunges. Pliés. Tendus.

On the uptown track across from me, two guys and a girl walk up the stairs and onto the platform. They peer into the tunnel, checking to see if a train is coming. One of the guys has short dark hair. The other one says something, and the short-haired boy smiles, shakes his head and looks down.

It's Ben. Not a fake one. The real one.

He's holding an instrument case, but it's bigger than a violin. I'm pretty sure it's a saxophone. The girl elbows him and he smiles at her, dimples flashing. I should be jealous, I should have rage burning inside me like I did with the red-haired girl, but for some reason I don't. There's an ease about him I've never seen before. Something has unwound. Not unraveled, but unwound.

Then he sees me, and our eyes meet across the platform, like there's an invisible thread pulling us tight through the empty space. I nod at his saxophone, and I can swear he nods back at my dance clothes. The corners of his blue eyes crinkle and I think I see his lips start to curve up into a grin.

An A train whooshes between us, and I flinch. I'm too close to the platform edge and I back up immediately. But it's an uptown train, on the opposite side, and it hesitates for a moment before the doors open.

Stand clear of the closing doors, please, echoes the recorded announcement. Then there's a ding and the doors shut again.

As the train pulls away, I hear the notes from *West Side Story.*

"There's a place for us ..."

I look back across the platform.

It's empty.

About the Author

Lindsay Champion is a graduate of the NYU Tisch School of the Arts, where she spent most of her time doing high kicks and eating falafel.

After a stint as a closed caption writer (best memory: captioning the first six *Rocky* movies for TV), she served as the features editor at Broadway.com, where she managed to interview her celebrity crushes Paul Rudd, Hugh Jackman and Jake Gyllenhaal without fainting or peeing her pants. She is the food and wellness director for the digital media company PureWow, mostly for the snacks.

This is her first novel.

Acknowledgments

When I was ten, my parents took their ancient typewriter out of the garage and put it on the curb to give away. I begged my dad to help me carry it upstairs to my room instead. My first YA novel, *The Sitter Sisters*, was a horrifically terrible knockoff of *The Baby-Sitters Club*. So my parents (mom: a children's book author; dad: a jazz musician and teacher) sat me down and explained the importance of finding my own creative voice. Mom, Dad, I can never thank you enough for doing this.

Fast forward to today: the incomparable Kate Egan is my editor. Ten-year-old me would be *flipping out* right now. Kate, you've made my experience as a first-time author an absolute dream. I'm so lucky to have you as my mentor, collaborator and guide, and I can't thank you enough for everything.

Without my brilliant agent Sarah Davies, this book would just be a stack of pages under my bed. She and the wonderful team at Greenhouse Literary Agency have never given up on me or my writing, even when I was *thiiisssscloooose* to giving up myself.

Huge thanks to Lisa Lyons Johnston, Genie MacLeod, Olga Kidisevic and the rest of the phenomenal team at KCP Loft for guiding me through this process and taking a chance on Dominique and Ben.

(And making this jaded New Yorker want to move to Toronto, because you're all so darn sweet and kind.)

My writing group buddies Michelle Levy and Amy Ball have seen every draft of this book, and they've helped me shape it from "wouldn't it be cool if I wrote something about a violin prodigy" to an actual *thing.* You guys rock.

Nicholas Pappone: a million thank yous for agreeing to meet with a writer you've never heard of in a tiny Italian restaurant in Washington Heights, bringing a stack of sheet music Ben would play and talking me through every last passage over wine and spaghetti. Thank you for fielding frantic phone calls about concertmasters and violin strings. Ben wouldn't exist without you.

A few more kind musicians have helped make sure Ben and the students at the Brighton Conservatory are as true to life as possible. Kevin Li, Janet Benton and Anthony "Hootz" Taylor, thank you so much for your help with these details.

I'm so grateful to my blondestorming partner Imogen Lloyd Webber for her help on the path to publication, Caitlin McNaney for connecting me to some fantastic music resources, Marc (not Mark) Snetiker for the endless support and Ryan Lee Gilbert for the killer book recommendations.

Grazie to lambs Jenny Anderson, Chelsea Nachman and Alyson Ahrns for being the best Italian vino-drinking companions (clearly, a lot of wine went into the making of this book).

Big thanks to the Electric Eighteens, Kim Turrisi and the KCP Loft authors for welcoming me into this community with open arms.

Thank you Kim Sarasohn for being a constant supporter of my work from day one, and for guidance regarding the psychological elements of this book.

William Thomashower, I'm hugely grateful for your legal advice and Broadway song stylings.

Linda, Pete, Gerry, Ellen, Noah, Jared, Masood, Bobak, Farzin, Sara, La'Jean and Juliet, you are the most amazing cheering squad.

Ryan, Mary Kate, Jillian, Susan, Gniaz, Dara and everyone at PureWow, thank you for allowing me the flexibility to write this book *and* be a part of the best team ever.

And Zhubin Parang. You make everything possible. I strive to be a billionth of the kind, patient, smart, loyal, understanding, caring, hilarious person you are. Thank you for believing in me, for punching up my dialogue and for being my on-demand neck masseuse.